THINGS THAT WILL NOT STAND

To Lucie

With Love

Nana

THE THINGS THAT WILL NOT STAND

MICHAEL GERARD BAUER

An Omnibus Book from Scholastic Australia

Omnibus Books
an imprint of Scholastic Australia Pty Ltd
(ABN 11 000 614 577)
PO Box 579, Gosford NSW 2250.
www.scholastic.com.au

Part of the Scholastic Group
Sydney • Auckland • New York • Toronto • London • Mexico City
• New Delhi • Hong Kong • Buenos Aires • Puerto Rico

First published in 2018.
Text copyright © Michael Gerard Bauer, 2018.
Cover design copyright © Astred Hicks, Design Cherry, 2018.

 A catalogue record for this
book is available from the
National Library of Australia

ISBN: 978-1-74299-758-2 (paperback)

Typeset in 11.5/17pt Caslon

Printed and bound by Griffin Press.
Scholastic Australia's policy, in association with Griffin Press,
is to use papers that are renewable and made efficiently from wood grown
in responsibly managed forests, so as to minimise its environmental footprint.

10 9 8 7 6 5 4 3 2 1   18 19 20 21 22 / 1

One for the Dudeists and dreamers.

1. THE UNSLIDING DOORS

I stare over at the glass sliding doors, willing them to open.

They don't.

Disappointing, but not surprising.

I check the clock on the wall to my right. Again. The glowing red numbers beam out that it's ten forty.

Five more minutes. Five more minutes and that's it. You have to draw the line somewhere, and I'm drawing it in five minutes' time. Which of course is exactly what I told myself at ten thirty and at ten thirty-five. But this time I'm serious. I *am*. Seriously. She either walks through those doors by ten forty-five or I'm out of here. And you can quote me on that. Quarter to eleven comes, I'm gone.

I gaze once more across the empty cinema foyer with its blue and gold-flecked carpet as a now familiar mantra starts cranking up in my head.

Walk through those doors. Come on. *Walk through those doors.* There's still time. The movie won't have started yet. There's sure to be a heap of ads. Always is. Plus trailers. And didn't that handout say something about some old black and white short showing first? So come on. It's not too late. *Walk through those doors.* Come *on.* Just this *one* time let something amazing happen for me. You can do it. You know you can. All you have to do is *walk through those doors*!

No one walks through the doors.

Depressing, but not surprising.

1

Right then, if that's the way it's going to be, I'm left with no choice. Time to unleash the fearsome power of my positive thinking. I'm desperate. Anything's worth a shot.

Before twenty more seconds pass she will walk through those doors. She will. She will walk through those stupid doors in the next twenty seconds.

I lock my eyes on the unsliding doors and commence a silent countdown from twenty. The lower I get, the slower I go. By the time I hit three, there are glaciers moving faster than I am. From three I inch my way to one. Then I squeeze out a few more precious drops of time before completing the final soul-crushing step to zero. Naturally, I have to spell it out.

Z … … E … … … R … … … … … … … … … … … … … … O.

No one walks through the doors.

A crock of shit, but not surprising.

Outwardly I don't react. But inwardly I'm dropping to my knees and delivering a gut-wrenching scream at the ceiling while being filmed from above.

Doing countdowns? Are you kidding me? This is what I'm reduced to? What am I? Sixteen or six? And who am I trying to fool, anyway? I mean when was the last time something incredible like I'm hoping for here actually happened to me?

BZZZZZ! Would the answer be … never?

Correct!

So why am I still standing around like a sad, pathetic dork holding this movie ticket and staring at these shitty wouldn't-slide-open-if-the-future-of-the-world-depended-on-it doors, expecting my crappy life to play out like one of those corny

'Very Ordinary Guy somehow manages to hook up with an Uber Amazing Girl', feel-good romcoms?

Why? Well, personally, I blame my mother. She was always watching those corny romcom movies when I was little. Not any more, of course. I think she's pretty much given up on happy endings now. But my point is, I watched a lot of them with her. And here's the thing. Watching those feel-good flicks, made me, well … feel good. I even liked *Love Actually*, actually. No, come to think of it, I actually loved it. There, I admit it. I'm a sad, pathetic dork and a traitor to my fellow raging hormones everywhere. So shoot me.

But even if I am a sad, pathetic dork, isn't it still possible for my real life to be like one of those feel-good movies? Not *all* the time, obviously, but maybe just *sometimes*. Like *now* for example. Couldn't I have my very own real-life, feel-good, romcom moment right here and right now? Just look around. The scene's all set. It's perfect.

You've got your loser-in-love Very Ordinary Guy (me) standing alone in a deserted cinema foyer with his eyes glued to a set of sliding doors, hoping and praying for them to open. Meanwhile time's ticking away, tension's building and it looks like our Very Ordinary Guy is on the brink of giving up. So all we need now for the feel-good overload to kick in is for the Uber Amazing Girl of his dreams to make her grand entrance.

Well, come on, then. Let's do this!

Lights. Camera. Quiet on set.

And *ACTION*!

And … nothing. Cue the crickets.

I check the time again. Ten forty-three. Great. Two minutes to go before my *final*, final deadline. Just one hundred and twenty short seconds left for my Uber Amazing dream Girl to appear and make my personal romcom fantasy a mind-blowing reality.

But could that happen? Could that *really* happen?

Well, I suppose so. But do you know what would make me just a teeny bit more optimistic? Two things, really.

1. If I'd found out what the Uber Amazing Girl's name was and

2. if I'd actually got around to asking her to go to the movies with me.

2. THE PERFECT FEMALE HUMAN

Yes, clearly I'm deluded. What other conclusion could you possibly come to?

But (and here's the crucial question I keep asking myself) am I totally, completely and absolutely deluded? Or is there still some slim sliver of hope that the Very Ordinary Guy hooking up with the Uber Amazing Girl scenario could possibly come true?

There's only one thing to do. Go back over everything that happened this morning and search for evidence of that elusive sliver. So let's see. Previously on *The Life and Times of a Very Ordinary Guy* …

It's the state university's Future Students Open Day, and like heaps of other mainly Grade Eleven and Twelve students our Very Ordinary Guy (yes, that would be me again) and his best friend Tolly have turned up during the mid-year break to try to decide what the hell their future courses and careers might be.

Soon after they arrive, Very Ordinary Guy and his friend split up. While his well-prepared and thoroughly researched colleague heads off to attend three different talks put on by the Science Department and the Medical Faculty, Very Ordinary Guy wanders through the milling crowds of students, parents and volunteers in the Main Exhibition Hall, then heads over to the Commerce Building with the vague idea of checking out the Business and Economics displays and hearing someone speak about Town Planning.

Just don't ask him why he's doing this. He's never really had any burning ambition to plan a town. In fact, it's been a while since he's had a burning ambition to do anything in particular. But his parents are happy about the idea and he figures that there'll always be towns. So there's that, right?

Anyway, after an hour or so of uninspiring display viewing, Very Ordinary Guy enters the lecture theatre where the Town Planning talk is being held. He finds himself a seat and passes the time reading the dozens of pamphlets that have been shoved into his hands by enthusiastic Open Day volunteers along the way. The theatre is fairly full, but there's still a single vacant seat to his right. Or there is, until someone squeezes past a line of protruding knees and asks, 'Is anyone sitting here?'

Very Ordinary Guy looks up. And sees a girl. She has light brown mid-length hair that sweeps across her forehead just above her blue almond-shaped eyes. She's wearing white shorts and a navy jumper with the words *New York* on the front. To save time, let's just say that she's basically perfect. Because basically she is. She is a PFH. A Perfect Female Human.

Very Ordinary Guy lets her know that the seat is free. He attempts to use actual words here but succeeds mainly in making some grunting and mumbling noises with his mouth and bobbing his head up and down like a deranged dashboard dog. Naturally that is the last piece of communication he expects to have with the new arrival, because as I have already pointed out, she is a Perfect Female Human, and Perfect Female Humans and Very Ordinary Guys simply don't get involved in extended exchanges. This is one of the great universal truths. A bit like gravity and the law for the conservation of energy.

She takes a seat. Very Ordinary Guy makes sure he doesn't stare at the PFH beside him but he can certainly sense the hum of her electric presence. Out of the corner of his eye he sees her take out a notebook and pen and start to write something at the top of the page. A second later he hears a sigh and then she's speaking to him. To *him*! A Very Ordinary Guy!

'Sorry, but you don't happen to have a pen I can borrow, do you? Mine's just died.'

He can't believe his luck. *Thank you, Lord of the Pen*, he says silently to himself.

Out loud he says, 'Sure. No problem,' and he digs into his backpack and pulls out a bulging pencil case, which he unzips and holds out towards her like an offering to a goddess. Which, of course, it pretty much is.

'Take your pick.'

She chuckles. Perfectly.

'Wow. Sure you brought enough?'

Straightaway Very Ordinary Guy realises how ridiculous and dorky he must appear to her. Who in the digital age has a collection of abandoned pens? Who even has a pencil case? Particularly one they've had since primary school? Of course he thinks of covering his embarrassment by making a joke or a witty remark, but that would mean he'd actually have to think of a joke or a witty remark, which under the pressure of being in close proximity to a PFH is *way* too many bridges, *way* too far.

So he chuckles back at her instead. Moronically.

She selects a pen and the following in-depth conversation follows.

'Thanks. I'll give it straight back at the end of the talk.'

'That's all right, keep it.'

'No, I'm fine. You can have it back.'

'I don't need it, really. I've got plenty.'

'You *sure*? It looks like a good one.'

'It's not. It's just a pen. I've got heaps more. And you'll need one for the rest of the day, anyway.'

'I can always buy one somewhere.'

'Don't bother. It's fine. No problem. Keep it.'

'Well, if you're sure …'

'I am. Really.'

'Okay. Thanks. But if you change your mind …'

'I won't. It's fine. It's yours.'

'Thanks.'

And they're done.

The truth is, Very Ordinary Guy would have offered her an entire stationery shop if he'd had one on him. He watches as she adds the date to the top of her page. She has neat, rounded writing. A Perfect Female Human is writing with one of his pens. What a time to be alive!

Very Ordinary Guy returns to shuffling through his pamphlets. They're from various university clubs and organisations, but it's the one from the university's cinema, the Hub, that catches his attention. Some recent mainstream movies are showing, but for Open Day the uni Film Club is also screening classic films and silent movie shorts. Among the classics are *On the Waterfront* starring Marlon Brando and *Casablanca* starring Humphrey Bogart and Ingrid Bergman.

This immediately catches Very Ordinary Guy's attention, because his friend Tolly's dad is a big film buff, and more than once he's claimed that *Casablanca* is 'as good as it gets'. Not only that, the day his friend's father found out that neither of them had even heard of *On the Waterfront*, he almost had a heart attack. 'What? You don't know *On the Waterfront*? Well, you haven't lived, boys! The taxi scene? Steiger and Brando? Best scene in the history of film. *You don't understand! I coulda had class! I coulda been a contender!*'

Very Ordinary Guy really likes Tolly's dad (which is one of the reasons he decided to do Film and Television at school this year) but he can't entirely vouch for his sanity. Anyway, he's still in his own little world thinking about all that when …

'Oooo, is that on today?'

The PFH is looking and pointing at the *Casablanca* ad. Her finger is touching the pamphlet he is holding. So indirectly she is touching him. And speaking to him. Again. A PFH is speaking to a Very Ordinary Guy when she has no real need to. She isn't trying to find a seat. She doesn't need a pen. She's just talking about wanting to see a movie. Talking to *him*. It's unprecedented. It's *exactly* the sort of scene Very Ordinary Guy would write for himself if he were to star in his very own feel-good, romantic comedy!

'*Casablanca*? Yeah, this morning. Ah … ten thirty,' he tells her.

'*Always* wanted to see that,' she replies. 'Seen bits of it online. Never the whole lot. And never on a big screen. That would be brilliant.'

'Yeah. Supposed to be good. Only five bucks too. Be worth going.'

'Hmmmmm. It would.'

And that's where the conversation ends, because while Very Ordinary Guy wastes precious time desperately trying to organise some passably intelligent words to come out his mouth in some sort of a logical order, a Town Planning lecturer takes her place behind the lectern and for the next half an hour everyone, including the PFH, has to listen to the words coming out of her mouth instead. Then as soon as the talk is over, the Perfect Female Human is immediately spotted and set upon by a couple of almost-as-perfect, haven't-seen-you-for-ages, long lost female friends, and she's bundled off in an excited bubble of chatter.

End of recap.

So that's it. That's what I'm pinning my hopes on. Not much. Or, to quote Tolly's dad, 'Just a bee's dick this side of zilch'.

What an idiot. Why couldn't I have said something when she mentioned about wanting to see *Casablanca*? Just something simple and non-threatening like, 'Well, I think I'm gonna go, so I might see you there.' That would have been enough. More than enough. That would have been brilliant. Who knows what she would have said in reply? And even if she'd said nothing, at least a sliver-of-hope seed would have been planted.

Of course, in the full romcom, fantasy version of our encounter the conversation would have gone like this: as soon as the PFH mentioned about wanting to see *Casablanca,* I would have flashed a suave, sophisticated smile at her and come out with, 'Of all the lecture theatres, in all the universities, in all the world, you walk into mine.' And that would have been it. Game over. That'll be two tickets, please. Here's looking at you, kid!

But unfortunately my real life always reads much more like a very badly written first draft rather than a polished final edit, so the few classic *Casablanca* lines I have stuck in my head, thanks to Tolly's dad, stayed well and truly stuck there.

Time for another clock check.

Ten forty-*six*.

Crap.

What a sad, pathetic prick you are, I silently remind myself, even though there's little chance of me ever forgetting.

I look down at the ticket stub in my hand. *Admit One.* Yep, that'd be right. Admit one sad, pathetic prick to the Sad Pathetic Pricks' Club. I'm about to rip it up and toss it in a nearby bin when some movement and a low rumble stop me.

I raise my head.

Across the foyer, the unsliding doors are sliding open.

And a girl is walking through.

3. THE HALF-FROZEN GIRL

Just not *the* girl.

Not the one I've been waiting for. Hoping for.

Not the PFH.

That'd be right. Of all the cinemas, in all the universities, in all the world, she *doesn't* walk into mine.

A lot of white. That's the first impression I get of the new girl. The *wrong* girl. She reminds me a bit of the main character from *Frozen* because her hair is bleached and falls in a jagged cut almost to her shoulders. Plus she's wearing white sandals that tie up above her ankles and a strappy white top that hangs loosely to a long white skirt. From my side view I can just make out a pale profile and an equally pale and slender arm.

What's her name again, that *Frozen* character? Something beginning with E, isn't it? Eva? Ellie? Evelyn? Something like that.

Doesn't matter.

The *Frozen* girl has stopped by a life-sized black and white cut-out of Humphrey Bogart. He's in a white tuxedo smoking a cigarette and standing beside a piano. The *Frozen* girl fits in with the colour scheme pretty well. I watch as she gives Bogie the once over then pulls out a purse from the calico bag she's carrying. The bag has those happy and sad theatre masks printed on it. I take one last pointless look at the clock on the wall and then the ticket in my hand to remind myself once more of my sad-pathetic-prick-like nature. When the

Frozen girl sets off for the box office, I move to intercept her.

'Are you getting a ticket for *Casablanca*?'

She stops and turns my way. She's a half a head shorter than me. And I realise now that she's also only half-*Frozen*. At least from the neck up. That's because the hair on the right side of her head is dark and shaved close and high over her temple. The ear on that side is almost hidden under a load of metal piercings. She pushes her long hair behind her other ear and holds it there. Grey-hazel eyes squint up at me from below dark, full eyebrows.

'Sorry,' she says, shaking her head slightly. 'What?'

'Are you going to see *Casablanca*? 'Cause if you are, you can have my ticket.'

I hold it up and she studies it for a second and then me.

'*Your* ticket? Why aren't *you* using it?'

Because I'm a sad, pathetic prick who actually thought for a moment that he might be like one of the leads in some heart-warming, feel-good romcom, but then quickly discovered that, no, he's just stuck in his regular pissy, feel-crap, non-romcom life after all.

I decide this might be oversharing, so I keep it to myself.

'Ah, I just … decided to … you know … do something else.'

'Really? What?'

'Sorry?'

'You said you decided to do something else. Well, what did you decide to do rather than see *Casablanca* even though you've already gone and bought a ticket for it?'

Her voice is husky and raw, like it's frayed at the edges. I don't mind the sound of it, but I hadn't expected to hear it

13

cross-examining me. I'm offering a free ticket here. I'm not selling life insurance or spiritual guidance. Why am I getting a grilling over it?

'Um, I don't know. Look, I just changed my mind about going to the movies. That's all.'

Her eyes become even squintier.

'Someone stand you up?'

'What?'

She's examining my face like some weird psychic seeking out telltale bumps and mysterious birthmarks.

'Yeah, you know what I think?' she says finally. 'I think you were expecting to go with someone or maybe *hoping* to, but they didn't show up and now you're all pissed off and want to get rid of your ticket because, hey, what sort of a loner-loser would even think of going to see a film all by themselves, right?'

She makes a sad face and points to the one on her bag at the same time. She's correct about one thing. I am pissed off. And she isn't helping.

'Sure, whatever. Look, do you want the ticket or not? If you do, it's yours for free. If you don't want it, fine. I'll just chuck it in the bin. I really couldn't care less either way.'

She nods slowly and points a black-fingernailed finger at me.

'You were *definitely* stood up, weren't you?' Then she quickly pushes a hand in front of my face to stop the words that are about to leap from my mouth. '*But* in answer to your question, yes, I will take your ticket. Can't let it go to waste. Thank you. *But* I'm paying for it.'

'You don't have to. Just take it.'

'I'm *paying* for it.'

She says that like she's beating the alternative to death with a hammer. Fine. What do I care? I give in and hand over the ticket and wait for her to sort out the money. While she's busy picking coins from her purse my eyes drift away. Then they lock on the scene unfolding behind her.

'Oh shiiiiii–it,' I say, not quite under my breath.

Across the foyer the sliding doors are opening again and a girl is walking through.

The girl this time.

4. THE DISASTER FILM

The half-*Frozen* girl stops digging around in her purse and looks to where I'm staring.

'That's her?' she asks. 'That's who you've been waiting for? Taylor Swift?'

I nod. Then frown.

'What? She doesn't look like Taylor Swift, does she?'

'Ah no, just totally.'

'Really? I can't see it.'

'Wow, so how long have you had this terminal case of face blindness?'

When I don't answer she drops the coins back into her purse.

'Well, I need to get going or I'll definitely miss the start of the movie. Hey, thanks a lot for the *Casablanca* ticket. Oh, and I've changed my mind and decided to take you up on the free offer. So generous of you. Bye!'

The expression on my face must be matching the thoughts exploding in my mind.

'Only joking,' she says. 'Congratulations. You are winning at life. And of course, now that … *Everything Has Changed* … you'll be needing this.'

For some reason she sings part of that last sentence.

'Did you see what I just did there?'

And before I can say that no, I actually didn't, she's pushed the ticket back into my hand and is continuing on her way to the box office.

I quickly turn back to *the* girl. She's just inside the sliding doors now, taking off her *New York* jumper and tying it around her waist. It looks like it was born to be there. After she straightens her hair and top, she does a quick scan around the foyer. When her eyes land on me, they pause.

And move on.

Okay. Not *quite* the reception I'd been hoping for.

I wait for the reverse pan to come my way. This time I force myself to throw up a dorky quick five-finger wave.

She sees it. There's a hesitation and a half smile. My heart does one of those lurching off a cliff and freefalling kind of things. A second later a proper smile lights up her perfect face and she picks up her bag and heads my way.

Oh my god. She's heading my way. It's happening. It's actually happening. My heart pulls out of its free fall and soars into the stratosphere. Ladies and gentlemen, we are now officially cruising in full romcom flight mode. Houston, we have no problem!

'Town Planning lecture, right?'

A PFH is standing right in front of me, smiling.

'Right.'

Then she stops smiling and a hand flies up to cover her mouth.

'Oh, and I've still got your pen, haven't I? Wait, it's here.'

She's about to start unzipping the multiple compartments in her designer backpack, but I stop her in time.

'No, no, it's okay. It's nothing. Don't worry. Please. Keep it.'

She lowers the bag to the floor.

'You sure? I know it's in there ... *somewhere*. Probably only take me ten, maybe fifteen minutes of frantic scratching around to find it. Twenty minutes at the most. Are you positive you don't need it?'

'Positive,' I tell her. 'If I ever have to buy a replacement I'll just quit school and get a job or rob a bank or something.'

Wow. Mild humour. Where did that come from? Nice job, brain and mouth!

She considers what I've said.

'Well, as long as you're not inconvenienced.'

And we both chuckle.

Did I say she was just a Perfect Female Human? I've undersold her. She's also smart and funny. And even more amazingly, she's being smart and funny with me. Aka Very Ordinary Guy.

'Oh, I'm Helena, by the way.'

'Hi. I'm Sebastian.'

I can't believe this. It could be dialogue plucked right out of one of my dream romcom movie scripts!

She glances over at the wall clock. Her profile is like something from a glossy magazine. I have to control myself from whipping out my phone and firing off a few shots.

'Hey, wasn't *Casablanca* supposed to start at ten thirty?'

'Yeah, but don't worry, there's always trailers and ads first and they're also showing some old silent comedy short I think, so if you get your ticket now you won't miss anything.'

Helena rolls her eyes and pushes a hand through her hair. It settles back into place. Perfectly.

'If only,' she says. 'But due to circumstances apparently beyond my control, I'm not going to *Casablanca,* am I? I'm going to the eleven o'clock session of *Fast and Furious* … *8* or *12* or whatever number it's up to now. And you know why? Because according to my boyfriend, "*Casablanca* sounds like a crap movie for old dudes and wankers".'

And suddenly my dream romcom world has been hit with a massive tidal wave and has morphed into a disaster film. Behind Helena the sliding doors are parting again. We both react to the sound.

'And right on cue, here he is,' she says.

The disaster deepens.

Helena's boyfriend joins us. He's wearing tight black jeans and a light blue T-shirt that someone has apparently painted on him. His hair is all gel and sharp angles with a part that looks like it's been cut with a laser beam. He makes brief eye contact with both of us before taking up a male-model menswear-catalogue pose beside Helena. Without speaking he snakes his arm low around her waist and simultaneously throws a battleaxe through my heart. Now I'm not sure if I'm in a disaster movie or some horror flick. Maybe both.

'Corban, this is Sebastian. We met in a Town Planning lecture this morning. Sebastian came to my rescue when my pen died. Sebastian, this is Corban, the well-respected film critic.'

Corban pulls a pained face at Helena and throws me a nod that seems to say, 'I can see that you are standing there, but you mean about as much to me as the carpet. Possibly less. Wait, make that *definitely* less.'

'Got tickets?' he asks Helena.

'No, I only just …'

Corban doesn't wait to hear any more.

'I'll get 'em,' he mumbles, and lopes his way catwalk-style to the ticket office.

Helena watches him go. She makes a face of exaggerated horror at me. It makes me wonder if there is any face she could pull that would stop her from being beautiful.

'It'd be so *terrible* if we missed the start of the film. How would we ever pick up the plot? *Unless* of course *Fast and Spurious 92* is basically the same as every other film in the franchise. But gee, what would be the chances of *that*?'

I give her my best sympathetic smile but inside I'm screaming, *Dump him! He's an arrogant knob. Come to* Casablanca *with me instead. We've gone way off script here. Someone call CUT! We have to get this whole romcom thing back on track. Now!*

But that doesn't look like it's going to happen any time soon. Instead, I become aware of Helena's smooth and flawless brow attempting to crease itself into a frown. Now she's pointing at the ticket in my hand.

'But hey, what about you? *You're* going to *Casablanca* and the session started almost twenty-five minutes ago. What are you doing hanging around out here? You waiting for someone?'

Yes, of course I'm waiting for someone. Isn't it obvious? You! I'm waiting for *you* to dump that arrogant knob and come with me.

'Well, I … um …'

My mind freezes. I'm not great at making things up on the spot. I need time to think everything through, see it from every possible angle, weigh up all the pros and cons and agonise over it before making what I always suspect is the wrong decision. And anyway, how am I supposed to answer her question? Do I say yes or no? If I say yes, then who will I say I'm waiting for and why aren't they here? If I say no, then she's right. Why *am* I still hanging around in the foyer?

'I'm just … well, I … you know … I was …'

And as I babble on saying nothing, Helena's perfect eyes begin to lose some of their happy sparkle and her perfect teeth slowly disappear behind the perfect lips of her now collapsing smile. A slide show of realisation, pity and embarrassment plays through on her face.

She's worked it out. Oh, god. She worked out the answer to her own question. She's staring into the eyes of a sad, pathetic prick and she knows it. And it's about to get worse. A lot worse. Because she's about to put that embarrassing knowledge into humiliating, ego-stomping words.

'Hey, I hope you weren't … I mean … I hope you didn't think … you know … that …'

My personal romcom/disaster/horror movie is now hurtling to its gut-wrenching climax. I wouldn't be at all surprised if it degenerated into an all-out slasher fest. And no prizes for guessing which Very Ordinary Sucker is going to be the prime slashee. I'm bracing myself for the inevitable onslaught when I catch a blur of white out of the corner of my eye and feel a body brushing in beside me.

'Phew! Got it. Sorry for holding you up.'

I'm staring at a half-shaved head and an ear full of shrapnel. The half-*Frozen* girl is standing next to me. She's waving a

Casablanca ticket about. I have no idea what's going on. Some kind of surprise twist, obviously. But what script is it from – romcom, disaster, horror, slasher? Or something else? Whoever's editing this thing is doing a lousy job!

The half-*Frozen* girl looks expectantly from me to Helena and back again. She's opening her mouth to speak. I'm desperately hoping that when she does, everything will make sense.

'So,' she says to me, 'you going to introduce us, or what?'

5. THE SANDPIT

Introduce you? Sure. Only I have no idea who you are!

Unfortunately, as usual, my mouth has already started up before my brain has had a chance to download any sort of a plan.

'Sorry. Yeah. Ah, this is Helena …'

Shit, now what? Wait. I just realised something. *I* don't know the name of the half-*Frozen* girl but then Helena doesn't know it either. That means I can say any name I want! I just have to come up with a girl's name. Any girl's name. Except now my mind has shut down and the only girl's name I can think of is Helena, and that one's taken already! Stall for time! Stall for time!

'… And aaah, Helena … this is … um …'

Come *on*. A name for the half-*Frozen* girl. Any name! And finally one drops from somewhere into my brain.

' … Elsa.'

Helena's eyebrows shoot skywards.

'*Elsa*. Really?' She laughs but then is immediately embarrassed and desperately tries to rein in the level of her surprise and disbelief. Meanwhile the half-*Frozen* girl beside me is screwing up her mouth and flinging narrow-eyed daggers at me.

'No. *Not* really.'

Then she ignores me to address Helena.

'Hi, it's *Frida*, actually.'

Now Helena looks totally lost. Still beautiful, but totally lost.

23

'I don't get it. What's with the different names?'

The girl who's introduced herself as Frida sighs and jabs a thumb my way.

'It's *this* one's idea of a joke. Whenever we meet someone new he likes to make up ridiculous names for me. Last time it was Khaleesi. Hilarious, isn't he? And sometimes when he's being even more obnoxious and painful than usual, he likes to pretend that he has absolutely no idea who I am. He finds this amusing, you see, because we've actually known each other for a really, *really* long time.'

'*Really?*' Helena asks with a chuckle. 'How long?'

She doesn't realise it, but she's not the only one interested in the answer to this question.

'Since kindergarten, actually. That's where we first met. In a kindergarten sandpit, to be exact. Can you believe it?'

Well, my answer is 'No way!', but it seems that Helena is more trusting.

'Wow. That's pretty amazing.'

'Yes, but it's what happens *next* that will shock you!' Frida announces in an exaggerated click-bait voice-over.

It works. Helena is totally hooked. And yes, I admit it, even I'm more than just a bit interested.

'Why? What happened?'

Frida gives me a nudge.

'Do you want to tell her or will I?'

What? What!

'Ah, no … you do it. You tell it so much better than me.'

'That's true. I do,' the Frida girl says with some pride. 'Well, what happened was, this guy right here … saved my life!'

Okay, now apparently we've totally left the very popular romcom/disaster/horror/slasher genre far behind and crossed over to the bizarre twilight zone of hard-core fantasy.

Helena's mouth has dropped open just a little. She looks like a kid who's just witnessed a magic trick, and another big chunk of my heart breaks away like a collapsing ice shelf.

'You're kidding?' she says.

'Well, "saved my life" might be a *bit* of an exaggeration,' Frida explains, 'but he did rescue me from Crazy Karen Kratzman, which is pretty much the same thing. Everyone at kindy was terrified of her. But not this guy. He stood up to her when she was picking on me and he made her stop. It was his first day too and he didn't even know me. We've been friends ever since.'

'Awwwww, BFFs,' Helena whines perfectly. 'That is so cute!'

'I know,' Frida says and pats my arm. 'My hero.'

I give them both the best sheepishly humble smile I can muster.

'What can I say? You do what you can.'

We are all still basking in the unbelievable 'cuteness' of Frida's fairy tale when Corban returns with tickets and enough popcorn, drinks and sweets to last the winter. Helena does another quick intro.

'Corban, this is Frida. Frida. Corban.'

Frida offers up a 'Hey' and Corban fires off one of his trademark nods.

'Corbs, can you believe that these guys met way back when they were in kindergarten?'

Corban's face is plastered with a look that says not only can he *not* believe that, but he can't for the life of him understand why he's even being told about it. In the end he ignores the question and thrusts his jaw at Helena.

'You ready?'

She claps her hands together.

'Sure am! *Fast and Furious* calls,' she says, then pulls a turned-down groper mouth look when Corban's not watching her. Nope. *Still* beautiful.

'Nice to meet you guys. Enjoy *Casablanca*. I'm sure *I* would have.'

Helena and Corban walk side by side down to the second cinema entrance. My potential leading PFH is exiting my life and there's nothing I can do about it. And to make it worse, she's taking my pen with her. My favourite one too. Roll the credits. That's all, folks! My light-hearted romcom/disaster/horror/slasher/fantasy movie has ended in tragedy. Who'd a thought? Well, me for a start.

'He doesn't deserve her,' Frida informs me.

'They never do,' I say.

She stares my way then waves her ticket under my nose again like smelling salts.

'Well, speaking of wallowing in self-pity and suffering from the pangs of unrequited love,' she announces cheerfully, 'Bogie's waiting.'

Might as well. I've already spent my five dollars, plus I've got time to kill before I'm supposed to meet Tolly for lunch. And, as an added extra, when Tolly's dad finds out I've seen *Casablanca* on the big screen, I know for certain he'll harass Tolly to death to make him watch it too. That's got to be worth something.

I follow the girl I now know as Frida into the darkened cinema. We enter at the back on the right-hand side. There are plenty of empty seats. Up on the screen the credits of the black-and-white short are rolling to the sound of a tinny piano. It looks like we've actually timed it perfectly. Frida trails a hand on the brick wall as she takes some careful steps down the aisle. She stops a few rows from the back.

'Well,' she whispers, casting her eyes around, 'do you want to sit together or do we sit separately and run the risk of looking like the kind of loner-losers who would go to see a film all by themselves?'

Frida's scratchy voice carries to a girl sitting alone just a couple of seats away. She freezes with half her arm lost inside an enormous carton of popcorn and aims a death-wish stare at us.

Frida holds up a hand and grimaces at her. 'Only joking,' she mouths.

The girl seems unconvinced.

I quickly guide Frida to an empty row further on and follow her as she makes her way to the middle. She chooses a seat and I sit beside her. We're only like that for about a second before she jumps up and swaps to the other side of me.

'Better view,' she explains.

As we're sitting pretty much dead centre and there's no one sitting in front of us, this doesn't make any sense to me at all. But I don't have time to think much before the intro to *Casablanca* starts. Frida settles back in her seat and, without taking her eyes off the screen, leans my way and speaks out of the side of her mouth.

'I just realised. I don't actually know your name.'

I lean her way and speak out of the side of my mouth.

'It's Sebastian.'

'Sebastian. Right. I'm Frida.'

'Yeah, I know,' I tell her. 'You probably don't remember me, but many years ago I actually saved your life in a kindergarten sandpit.'

The half-*Frozen* girl beside me taps a finger on her lips and raises an eyebrow.

'I *thought* you looked familiar,' she says.

We're both smiling as the movie starts.

6. THE FEMINIST ICON

Frida and I watch *Casablanca* from beginning to end in silence. The next time we speak is outside in the foyer.

'Well, what did you think?' she asks me.

'Yeah, I liked it. Different. Bit old-fashioned and corny at times, but I'm glad I've seen it now.'

'What did you like best about it?'

'There were some great lines, and Bogart was cool. Can't believe that ending though. I mean he *finally* gets the girl back but then he tells her to leave him behind and get on the plane with the other dude instead. And she does!'

Seriously. What kind of story is that? I knew it wasn't a 'com' but I was expecting just a touch more 'rom'.

'But that's the best part,' Frida informs me. 'Don't you see? Bogie gives up Ilsa for her own good and for the good of the cause. He realises that Victor is the better man for her and the safer option. So he does the right thing. It's a selfless and noble act. It's beautiful. He sacrifices the great love of his life and stays behind with Louis instead, to fight the good fight.'

She pauses then.

'Think of it as a bit like how you really wanted to go to the movies with Taylor Swift but ended up going with me instead. So she was like Ilsa to your Bogie.'

I can't say I'm entirely with her, although I'm totally okay with being compared to Humphrey Bogart.

Now she's frowning.

'Which I suppose makes *me* Louis.'

Frowning harder now.

'Except of course, *you* didn't really have any choice, did you? You were *forced* to give up your Ilsa. So there was nothing really selfless or noble or beautiful in anything you did, was there? So yeah. I take it back. The two things are actually *totally* different and you're nothing like Bogie at all.'

I wait a second for my head to stop spinning.

'Gee, thanks for explaining that all to me,' I say finally. 'I feel *so* much better about myself now.'

'No problem,' she replies with a smirk.

I'm not sure what to do or say next. Around us the foyer is emptying rapidly. I check the time. A quarter to one. Frida notices.

'So what are your big plans for the rest of the day?'

'Nothing much. Supposed to meet my mate Tolly in the cafeteria soon to get something to eat. Then we're going to check out the drone battles that the Engineering students are putting on in the Great Court at one thirty. After that, I'm not sure. Knowing Tolly, there'll still be people he'll want to talk to or something he'll want to see. I'll probably just wander around checking out stuff till we get picked up sometime after five. What about you?'

'There's a theatre sports demonstration that I want to go to. It's on at the same time as that drone thing. Probably meet a bunch of friends there. Then, yeah, same as you. See what else there is to see. They've got those bands playing in the Great Court from around six so I might stick around for a bit of that.

Not sure. It depends on how I'm feeling. And what my friends are doing. Right now I'm starving.'

'Yeah, me too.'

We look at each other.

'Well … you can always … you know … come get something with Tolly and me. If you want to. Up to you.'

Frida considers the carpet for a second or two then lifts her head.

'Yeah, sure. Why not? I've never met a Tolly before. It will be a new experience for me.'

'Ooooh, it definitely will,' I assure her. 'I can guarantee you that.'

The cafeteria is busy and noisy, so after we buy our lunch we follow Frida's suggestion and find a table out on a side terrace. Her with her coffee, muesli bar and sushi rolls and me with my orange juice, toasted sandwiches and hot chips. I bite into two slices of crisp bread oozing with melted cheese, tomato and ham and nudge the carton of chips to the centre of the table.

'Help yourself.'

'Thanks, but I might see how I go with these first.'

The conversation is put on hold then as we both concentrate on attacking our food. It gives me the opportunity to really look at the girl sitting opposite me while she's focused on eating. As well as the attention-grabbing things like her hair, her piercings and the fact that she has black fingernails on one hand and white on the other, I notice smaller details about her. Things like the light sprinkle of freckles on her cheeks, the way her mouth drops down just a little at the ends, the thinness of her lips and the faint scar across the bridge of her nose. It's an interesting face. The kind of face that doesn't reveal its secrets all at once.

A small bird lands on the table beside us and Frida turns to watch as it pecks at a few scraps of bread. Her right ear, the one crowded with piercings, is now facing my way. I'm studying the various rings and studs and other bits and pieces when a pair of grey-green eyes catches me in the act.

'What is it?'

'Sorry. Just checking out all your piercings and stuff. Those little moons are cool.'

Four small silver discs showing the phases of the moon from crescent through to full are dangling on tiny chains from the fleshy part of her lobe. She runs a finger through them and they twist and swing about.

'They're new,' she says. 'Supposed to remind me that things can change.'

It seems like a strange thing to say.

'You need reminding?'

'More like convincing,' she says almost as an aside before she goes back to her sushi rolls. Since that line of conversation appears to be over, I try another one.

'Hey, thanks for what you did. You know, back at the theatre. Covering for me so I didn't look like a complete loser.'

Frida takes a sip from her coffee and places it down on the table.

'Well, when I saw the boyfriend appear, I figured that wasn't *exactly* part of your plan.'

'No. Not exactly.'

I feel myself being observed. Assessed even.

'So … you didn't *know* she had a boyfriend?'

Confession time.

'Nope. Only spoke to her for about three minutes before a talk this morning. She borrowed my pen. Didn't even get a chance to ask her name.'

Frida tilts her head sideways as if looking at me from a different angle might somehow help her to make more sense of that last piece of information.

'You asked her to go to the movies with you … and you didn't even know her name?'

'Ah, well you see, I didn't *actually* ask her to go to the movies with me. At least, not in so many words.'

'How many words then?'

'Well, if I round them up … none.'

On the other side of the table Frida pushes out her bottom lip and she stares with dead eyes like someone who's been cracked on the back of the head with a blunt object and is now mildly concussed.

'Riiiiiight. So let me see if I have this correct. You didn't know her name or really anything about her, you didn't ask her to go see a movie with you … and *yet* … you were there waiting for her to show up?'

'Yup,' I say, making a popping sound with my lips. 'That's it in a nutshell. And I emphasise the word *nut*.'

'Well, that's … just … weird.'

I think about trying to defend myself, but then decide that

she's probably hit the weird nail right on its weird head. When it becomes clear that I'm not going to challenge her statement, she continues.

'So anyway, you looked like you were about to drown in a sea of embarrassment, so I thought I'd try to throw you a lifeline.'

'Perfect image,' I tell her. 'And thanks for the lifeline. I needed it.'

I take another chunk out of my toasted sandwich then remember something.

'Not sure I needed that "aren't you going to introduce us" bit though.'

'Oops. Sorry about that,' she says without any attempt to look sorry at all. 'Couldn't help myself. Just wanted to see what you would do.'

Then she pulls a face like she's bitten into a sour lemon.

'But *Elsa*? Really? A cartoon character? That's the best you could come up with? Of all the millions of possible girls' names at your disposal, you couldn't think of something a little more believable or a little less ridiculous and obviously made up, than that?'

'Hey, I panicked, all right? I'm not great at being spontaneous. I was under pressure and I don't work well under pressure. It's just what came into my head, okay? Anyway, not much chance of me coming up with Frida, was there?'

She acts like she's insulted.

'Why not? What's wrong with Frida? You don't think I look like a Frida? I'll have you know I'm named after Frida Kahlo. Although you probably have no idea who that is.'

34

Ha! She's wrong. I do, actually. Someone in my class gave a talk on Frida Kahlo for an English assessment piece last year. I point at my forehead.

'The eyebrow woman?'

A half-eaten sushi roll drops from Frida's hand and lands on her plate and I sense almost immediately that I am in trouble. She pushes her lips forward to form a pinched O-shape. Then the O-shape begins to expand.

'Wow,' she says slowly and deliberately, and then repeats it as if once wasn't quite enough to cover the magnitude of the wow-factor she is experiencing. 'Wow. I am *so* impressed. No, really I am. All *most* people know about Frida Kahlo is trivial stuff like how she created all this unique and amazing art and about her role as a feminist icon. But not you. No, you have really zeroed in on her greatest achievement of all, haven't you? Facial hair. Well done. That makes you our carry-over champion.'

Cruel *and* unfair!

'Hey, I actually *did* know about some of that other stuff, okay, but I just thought …'

'Thought what? That "Eyebrow Woman" really summed up the *essence* of her contribution to humanity? Is that what you were going to say?'

I decide that this is an argument I'm never going to win, so I munch on a few chips and take a swig of juice to stop myself talking for a while. Then I wisely change the subject.

'So what about that story you made up, then? The one about me saving you from that kindergarten bully? What was that all about?'

Frida stabs one of her white-tipped fingers my way and drills me with her eyes.

'So, at long last you admit it, do you? You admit that what I said never actually happened. You admit that *you* didn't rescue *me* that day in the sandpit, but that *I* rescued *you*.'

Frida sighs heavily then like she's fed up with the whole thing.

'You know, I actually thought that after all these years of being BFFs you might have found the courage to finally face up to the truth. But it seems I was sadly mistaken.'

She retrieves what's left of the sushi roll from the plate, drops it into her mouth and starts chewing.

Right. I get what she's doing here.

'Well, why don't you tell me *your* version of the events, then? Please, enlighten me.'

'Gladly. It was your first day at kindy, but what *really* happened was that Crazy Karen Kratzman stole one of your lunch sandwiches and you stupidly ran after her and told her to give it back. Which she did. But only after she took it to the sandpit, added an extra filling of actual sand, and told you to eat it. When I got there you were sobbing away and half-choking on a mouthful of sand-sandwich. Oh, and you'd also wet your pants. Big time. I can still picture that enormous, wet patch on the front of your shorts. Mainly because it reminded me of the Batman symbol. Only made of urine.'

I stare across the table at her. She stares back. She wins.

'What a great story,' I say. 'Thanks for sharing. And so then you saved me – how, exactly?'

'First I turned a hose on Crazy Karen. Thought water might have a calming effect. Got *that* completely wrong, didn't I? She and I ended up mud-wrestling in the sandpit. I made her swallow quite a bit of it before they pulled me off. She didn't bother you after that. Not while I was around. Then she was banned from kindy a few days later, so you were safe. And *that's* how we became BFFs. You can formally thank me now if you like.'

She throws a big cheesy smile my way, revealing two rows of neat but slightly crooked small, white teeth. I smile back. Two can play at crazy.

'Well, I *would* thank you, if any of that was even remotely true. But sadly the passing of time must have somewhat dulled and distorted your memory of what *really* happened in the kindergarten sandpit that fateful day.'

Frida's eyes light up and her dark eyebrows arch.

'Is that so? Fascinating. Do tell.'

'Love to. You see, *my* recollection is that it was *you* who was forced to eat the infamous sand-sandwich. There may also have been pants wetting, but I'm far too much of a gentlemen to mention it. Anyway, then *I* came along, took Crazy Karen gently aside and explained to her that what she was doing was totally unacceptable in a civilised society and I encouraged her, from that moment on, to strive to be the very best person she could possibly be.'

'Really? And how did that work out for you?'

'Like a charm. Crazy Karen broke down in tears and apologised for her bad behaviour and promised to change her evil ways. It was quite something. I'll never forget the deafening applause and cheering that broke out in the playground when you and Crazy Karen hugged and wept in each other's arms. So moving. And as I'm sure you would recall, for my heroic efforts I was awarded the Junior Gandhi Peacemaker of the Week badge. Plus a gold star.'

Frida shakes her head at me with her mouth clamped into a straight line.

'You know, it's really sad to see someone *so* delusional, *so* misguided and so *totally* divorced from reality,' she says.

I shake my head in sympathy with her.

'Isn't it just.'

7. THE TOWN PLANNER

We go back to mostly silent munching for a few minutes until Frida finishes her coffee and pulls a water bottle from her bag.

'So. Okay. What school do you go to, then? And what grade are you in?'

She asks the questions like it's some ritual she's expected to perform.

'St Jerome's. Grade Eleven. You?'

'No, not me. I go to an entirely different school.'

I reward her joke with my own version of Corban's pained look, but secretly I think it's not too bad.

'And what school would *that* be, then?'

She takes a quick swig from her water bottle before she answers.

'Kingston Girls College. Grade Eleven too.'

I'm familiar with Kingston girls with their long green pleated skirts, regulation green hair ribbons, blazers and hats. It's hard to imagine multiple earrings and partly shaved hair fitting in too well there. I think about saying something but more questions start coming my way.

'So what are you thinking of doing at uni? Been to any talks, or have you just been hanging around the Hub hoping that random girls will rock up and want to go to the movies with you?'

'Very funny. But I'm not really sure what I want to do. Don't even know if I'll be coming here. If I did, then I'd maybe do something in Business Administration. Probably Town Planning.

I went to a talk on that.'

This pulls Frida up mid-chip grab.

'Town Planning? Okay. That sounds … like something people do. Why that?'

'Dunno, really. There'll always be towns, I guess, so it'd be pretty secure career-wise.'

It's clear from her face that my reasoning doesn't excite her much.

'Right. Of course there'll always be shit too, so maybe you should consider a future in sanitation.'

Ouch. It's probably a valid point, but I can't let her get away with it.

'You know, surprisingly enough, *that* was my first career option. But then I figured that for someone with my ability and talent, sanitation would appear to be such a … *waste*.'

Frida's eyes roll to the heavens like she's suddenly lost the will to live.

'Aaaargh! That is *so* bad. You should get down on your knees and apologise to the Comedy Gods for coming up with a *crap* joke like that.'

'It'll be fine,' I assure her. 'I'm sure they realise that I was just being … *faeces*-tious.'

Boom! Tish! Gold-coated gold! Somebody should be writing this stuff down for future generations. Although the face across the table doesn't appear to agree with me.

'You done now? Or do you have some more *shitty* puns that you feel the need to *push out* before we move on?'

Game on.

'Well, I was going to mention something about me being unde-*turd* by your criticism, but I'm happy to, you know … *let it go.*'

'Good,' she says. 'I'm *relieved.*'

We both eye each other closely and fight off the urge to smile. Frida picks up a long chip, dips it in some sauce and bites it in half.

'So tell me, then. Did that talk you went to fire up your inner town planner? Did you feel like racing home and whipping up the designs for a shopping mall or maybe an integrated transportation network?'

'Not really,' I reply, ignoring the sarcasm. 'Look, I didn't say I was definitely doing Town Planning, did I? I'm still trying to make up my mind, which is why I'm here. Anyway, what about you, then? I suppose you've got everything worked out, have you?'

Frida chews on her chip and nods.

'Uh-huh. Pretty much. Arts degree with majors in English Literature and Creative Writing. Hopefully a Psychology major too. Maybe eventually a full Psychology degree. Went to a Psych talk and a Creative Writing talk and spent the rest of the morning talking to tutors and lecturers and undergraduate students over at the English Department display. So good. Got heaps of information. That's why I was running a bit late getting to the movies.'

'So what would you do after uni with all that? What sort of job do you want?'

'A writer of some sort.'

If the BFF sandpit saga was anything to go by, I couldn't see her having much trouble making stuff up.

'And Psychology? Why that?'

'Just always been interested in people and why they do the things they do. You know, like what goes on in their heads and how they become what they are. Be good for my writing too. Help me understand my characters better and what motivates them.'

'Hard to earn a living from writing, isn't it? If you got that Psychology degree would you try to get a job in counselling or psychiatry or something like that first?'

'Doubt it,' she says, as if just the suggestion left a bad taste in her mouth. 'I've had a gutful of counselling and therapy.'

There's an awkward pause, which stretches on for a couple of seconds before her laughter puts a stop to it.

'No, I'm not crazy. It's my dad. *He's* a psychiatrist, so it feels a bit like I've been analysed twenty-four/seven my whole life. At least my mum's more normal. She's an artist. A painter mainly. She's the one who chose my name. God knows what Dad would have called me. Sigmund, probably. Anyway, counselling and therapy are not my thing. I'm more like Mum. I need something more creative. Might give Town Planning a big miss too while I'm at it.'

Another dig at me. It was starting to get a little annoying.

'Hey, just because someone decides to do something like Business Administration or Town Planning doesn't mean they can't be creative and have other interests as well, you know. You *are* allowed to have different sides to your character.

Just because you don't *happen* to be a full-time writer or an artist or something, it doesn't mean you're boring and one-dimensional.'

Frida holds her hands in front of her face as if to ward off an assault. She peeks out from behind them and flashes her small and slightly wayward teeth at me.

'Whoa, sorry. Didn't mean to offend you. And I agree. People can have different sides to them.'

The conversation dies for a bit then, until Frida puts her elbows on the table and locks her fingers together to form a little bridge that she rests her chin on. Her eyes are levelled at me.

'So, do *you*?'

'Do I what?'

'Have different sides to your character? Other interests outside the fascinating realms of Business Administration and Town Planning? More creative ones, perhaps?'

'Yeah. I guess. Sure.'

'Like what?'

I know she said that counselling and psychiatry weren't for her, but right now it feels a lot like she's my therapist and I'm her patient. Like father, like daughter, I guess.

'I don't know. I like music – same as everyone. I play guitar. Watch a lot of movies. I like doing Film and Television at school. I read a fair bit too when I get time.'

I'm not sure whether I should go on or not, but her eyes never leave me, and for some reason I feel I have to prove something more to her.

'I write some stuff.'

43

And her head bobs up like a trap that's been sprung.

'Oooh,' she says, narrowing her eyes, 'the town planner is a closet writer. *Now* you've got me hooked. Tell me more.'

'I didn't claim to be a writer. I just scribble down random stuff when I feel like it. It's rubbish mostly.'

'What kind of stuff? Where? How? Come on, out with it. I want a full confession with all the details. Leave nothing out.'

There seems to be no escape, so I take a deep breath and dive in.

'Okay, I have these diaries. More like journals, I guess. My mum buys me one every Christmas as part of my present. She started doing it when I was little.'

'Cute,' Frida says, without much emotion.

'Yeah, well, I used to just write about the things I did each day. But now I use them to jot down whatever I'm thinking. Or feeling. Could be anything. Usually it's just a few lines. But longer stuff too. Sometimes it turns into a kind of a poem. Sometimes song lyrics. But there's a lot of crap. And a lot of blank pages too.'

Frida whistles softly.

'Poetry and song lyrics, hey? You better hope the Council of Town Planners Standards Committee doesn't hear about this. You could be dragged before an inquiry to explain yourself.'

She thinks about it a bit more.

'Unless of course you only write songs and poems about the joys and sorrows of things like high-density housing. That would probably be allowed.'

'*Again* with the Town Planning put-downs?'

'Sorry,' she says, with no sincerity behind it. Then her face lights up like someone has flicked a switch. 'Hey, recite one of your poems for me or maybe sing a bit from one of your songs.'

I stare at her. She doesn't appear to be joking or to have temporarily lost her mind. But the idea itself is so ridiculous that it makes me laugh.

'No way. My poems aren't for public consumption, and anyway, I'd need a guitar to play you a song. Even then I wouldn't do it.'

'What, so nobody's ever heard any of your poems or songs?'

'Nope. I'm the only one who's had to suffer for my art.'

I can see that Frida is super keen to press me further, because her mouth is already half opened, but she's cut short by a towering male figure who has appeared at our table. We both stop and strain our necks to gaze up at him.

The new arrival is thin and well over six feet tall, but his hair, which is an explosion of curly, black sausage-shaped ringlets, makes him appear even taller. He's wearing black jeans and T-shirt and a loose-fitting op-shop tweed jacket with big oval elbow patches. Dark eyes study us through black-framed glasses. He scratches at the beard stubble on his chin and waits a good few seconds before he speaks.

'We've had numerous complaints from our other patrons regarding the excessive drug use, offensive language and obscene behaviour at this table.'

I check Frida's reaction. She's observing him closely, like she's dissecting him and peeling back the layers with her eyes.

'Complaints, eh?' she says at last. 'Well, you know what *you* need to do? You need to tell those other patrons to back off and get a life.'

The new arrival considers this for a split second, then addresses the people seated around us.

'Hey, back off, you lot, and get a life!' he shouts, much to their surprise and confusion.

He returns his attention to us and waits.

'Frida,' I say, 'meet your very first Tolly.'

8. THE BEST FRIENDS

Tolly drags over a spare seat from a nearby table, plants himself between the two of us and starts tucking in to my chips. At the same time, he pushes his glasses back over the bridge of his nose and points from Frida to me and back again.

'What is the meaning of this?' he asks.

I'm happy to explain.

'Well, Tolly, this is Frida, and you might be surprised to learn that Frida and I first met a *very* long time ago – way, way back in a kindergarten sandpit in fact – and guess what, I saved her life there and we've been BFFs ever since.'

Tolly's chip-chomping pauses only long enough for him to say one word.

'Interesting.'

'And here's something else you'll find interesting. We've just been to see *Casablanca* at the uni cinema.'

Now Tolly has stopped chomping and is pointing a long, bony finger my way.

'Which is something you will not mention to you-know-who under pain of death.'

'We'll see,' I tell him, with as little reassurance as I can possibly muster.

I notice Frida's confusion.

'Tolly's dad,' I explain. 'Big film nut. Always trying to get us to watch his favourite movies with him. Especially really old ones like *Casablanca*. Got this massive collection. Calls it the

Repository of Movie Awesomeness.'

'Interesting,' Frida says, imitating Tolly.

Tolly turns to her.

'Frida? As in Frida Kahlo?'

She looks pointedly at me before answering.

'Yes. You know about her?'

Tolly looks off into the distance and speaks like some data signal is being beamed directly through him.

'Mexican artist. Born early nineteen hundreds. Famous for her self-portraits. Significant political and feminist figure. Had polio and a serious traffic accident when she was young, resulting in long-term health problems. In a fairly fiery marriage. Can't remember her husband's name. Wait, someone Romero. No, Rivera, I think. Yeah, definitely Rivera.'

Frida gives him a sympathetic smile.

'Well, not a *bad* effort, I suppose, but sadly you didn't do *quite* as well as Sebastian here, who of course didn't bother with all the *trivial* details that you mentioned and totally nailed Frida Kahlo as the Mother of the Mono-brow.'

The lopsided smile on Tolly's long, thin face indicates that this doesn't surprise him in the least. He nods his head, which makes his black sausage curls wiggle and flop about.

'As you no doubt have observed, our Sebastian is a very, very impressive young man,' he says, and scoops up some more chips.

Of course Tolly knows more about Frida Kahlo than me. Tolly knows more about most things than me. In fact, I'd go so far as to say that Tolly knows more about most things than most people. I don't think that makes him a genius or anything, but he's pretty much a certainty to be Dux next year. Probably school captain too if he wanted it. And if it was just up to the student vote.

Another chip is about to disappear into Tolly's sizeable mouth when it wins a last-second stay of execution and remains dangling from his fingers.

'But here's what I find somewhat perplexing, Frida. Sebastian says that you two met in a sandpit? In kindergarten?'

'Correct,' Frida replies with a confident smile as if she's up for the challenge that she knows is coming.

'*And* that you've been best friends ever since?'

'Also correct.'

'Well, Frida, this is the source of my confusion. You see, *I've* known Sebastian ever since we started at St Jerome's Primary together in Grade Four and *yet* until now, not only have you and I never met, but not once has Sebastian ever mentioned you to me. Now, don't you find that all … rather strange?'

Frida's pale hazel eyes hold Tolly's gaze while a tiny, concerned fold forms between her eyebrows.

'Now that you put it like that, Tolly, yes, I definitely do. I do find that rather strange. And not only that, I think you deserve an explanation.'

This should be good. I can almost see Frida's creative writing mind churning over story possibilities. I'm actually keen to hear what she'll conjure up to get herself out of this.

'In fact I think we *both* deserve an explanation,' she adds before redirecting her eyes my way. 'Well, Sebastian? We're waiting. What have you got to say for yourself? Why is it that, after all these years, you have never once introduced me to your … *second*-best friend here? Or mentioned him to me? Are you ashamed of him or something?'

Now Tolly's head is also twisted my way. He rests a cheek on his fist and mirrors Frida's creased forehead.

'Come on, Mister Possible Future Town Planner,' she says, throwing down the challenge. 'Show us what you've got.'

She's trying to fire me up. And it's working.

'Gladly,' I tell her, without any idea what I'm going to say next. Both Frida and Tolly lean in a little.

'Well … I'm very pleased that you asked me that question. Really pleased. In fact I've been wanting to explain this whole thing to you both for quite some time because I'm … um … sick of leading a double life.'

'Then here's your big chance,' Frida says with a mocking grin. 'Unburden yourself. Get it *all* off your chest.'

'Fine. I will. The truth is that I wanted you two to meet for years, but I couldn't let it happen … because … because of *something* that occurred … in Grade Three. I'm sure you remember *that*, don't you, Frida? The thing that occurred in Grade Three?'

She flaps a hand at me.

'Of course I remember the *thing* that occurred in Grade Three. How could I forget the *thing*?'

'Great. You want to tell Tolly about it?'

'Nuh.'

Why am I not surprised?

'Okay then, *I'll* tell him.'

'I'm all ears,' Tolly says.

'Yes, we know, but your delightful personality more than makes up for it,' I say.

Frida squishes up her lips to stop herself from smiling. It makes me feel good. I go on.

'Anyway, it was back in Grade Three ... like I said ... and Frida and I were in the same class ... that would be Grade Three, of course ... and everything was totally fine until ...'

I'm scratching around for inspiration when I notice the jar of little sugar packets on the table.

'... until Billy Sugar showed up.'

'Billy Sugar,' Frida says, plucking one of the sachets from the jar. 'Ah, yes. I remember him well. Such a *sweet* boy.'

Tolly and I wince at her but we refrain from groaning out loud. Somewhere in her comment I find a flash of inspiration.

'Well, Frida,' I continue, 'you might say that *now*, but back in Grade Three it was a very different story – as you well know. Things were pretty sweet for a while, but then they quickly turned sour when Billy Sugar and I became friends and you were consumed with jealousy.'

Frida looks unconvinced.

'Consumed with jealousy? Over you and Billy Sugar?'

'Yes. That's right. You accused me of liking him more than you. You claimed I was obsessed with him. Actually, wait, now that I think of it, your exact words were, "Sebastian, you're addicted to Sugar!"'

I watch with some satisfaction as two pairs of eyes glaze over and are rolled in unison at me.

'Then you warned Bobby …'

'Billy.'

'Thank you, Tolly. I was getting Billy Sugar mixed up with Bobby Honey. Another really sweet kid. I think they were cousins.' More eye rolls. 'But as I was saying, you were so jealous, Frida, that you warned *Billy* to stay away from me – or else. Eventually you just went … too far.'

I lower my head and close my eyes for dramatic effect. I chew on my thumbnail. It's one of life's great tragedies that members of the Academy aren't watching.

Tolly places a hand on my arm. 'Can you talk about it?' he asks gently.

I mumble that I'll try, and I struggle on.

'One day when the bell rang for lunch, the teacher dismissed us and all the class went outside. All the class except Billy Sugar, that is. Billy didn't move. He didn't move because he *couldn't* move. Someone had covered his chair in super glue! It was horrible. Not only were his pants stuck but because he'd been sitting there so long, the glue had seeped through to his skin.'

I pause to compose myself.

'Poor, sweet, Billy Sugar had to be taken to hospital by ambulance – with a chair still attached to his backside. And even though that meant he had no trouble at all finding a seat in the waiting room, it didn't make up for him having to endure the horrific process of hydrochloric acid being applied to his rear end *and* parts of his genitals, in order to remove the offending piece of furniture.'

Beside me Tolly sucks in some air sharply through his teeth.

I can see his A+ Chemistry mind ticking over.

'Hydrochloric acid to dissolve glue, you say? Well, I'm no doctor, but it wouldn't have been my first choice.'

'I know it sounds incredible, Tolly, but you have to remember that these were less enlightened times.'

'Of course,' Tolly says. 'Eight years ago. Practically the Dark Ages. And so, just to be clear, Sebastian, are you saying that the person who perpetrated that heinous, super glue crime was …'

He doesn't say her name but he pulls his glasses down and his eyes dart sideways to Frida while he thrusts his head wildly in her direction.

'Well, Tolly, *officially* they never found the culprit, but I do have my very strong suspicions. Which is why, when I started at St Jerome's the next year and *we* became friends, I thought it was best for your own safety that I keep *you* a secret from …'

I stare across the table and imitate Tolly's wild head-thrusting at Frida.

'Riiiiiiight,' Frida says, her voice as flat and chilled as an ice rink. 'And I suppose you didn't tell *him* about being friends with *me* because you thought he'd be consumed with jealousy too. Is that it?'

I give her my best what-in-the-world-are-you-talking-about? look.

'No. Not at all. I knew that Tolly would be perfectly okay with me having a friend, because after all Tolly is a perfectly reasonable and mature human being. No, I had to keep you a secret from Tolly, not because you and I were friends, but because you were … a girl.'

Tolly's head goes up like he's been jabbed in the back. He adjusts his chair with a screech so that it is facing even more towards me, and folds his arms. But it's Frida who asks the question.

'You kept me a secret from Tolly because I was a *girl*?'

'You probably still are,' I suggest helpfully. 'But yes, that's what I'm saying. You see, ever since I've known Tolly – and I'm sure he won't mind in the least me telling you this – he's had this crushing and debilitating phobia about the opposite sex. Why, back in primary school the mere mention of a girl would start him sweating, dribbling and hyperventilating. If one came close to him or spoke to him, he'd break out in a very nasty rash in the … groinal region. Fortunately, in Tolly's case, that's not such an extensive area.'

Frida's lips squeeze together again like a little pink accordion. Tolly's face, meanwhile, is looking like one of those Easter Island statues, except not quite so amused. He holds up a finger.

'Before you continue with this *fascinating* tale, Sebastian, can I just have it recorded in the minutes that this will not stand?'

'Duly noted,' I say.

Frida looks confused again, but I don't have time to explain.

'In any case,' I say, 'I hope you understand now why I've been so determined to keep you both apart. But what a nightmare it's been! Making separate arrangements with each of you and keeping track of where you both were, so your two worlds wouldn't collide. It's been hell. Finally, I decided it couldn't continue any longer.'

I fold my arms and rest my elbows on the table. I look at Frida and Tolly in turn.

'You see, I realised that after Grade Twelve all three of us could, in all probability, end up here at this university, where it would be impossible to maintain my charade. My only course of action therefore was to bring you together *beforehand* and hope that both of you had finally reached a level of maturity that would allow *you*, Frida, to overcome your understandable but insanely destructive jealousy, and *you*, Tolly, to confront your childlike but disturbing sexual hang-ups.'

I push myself back and sit tall in my seat for the big finish. I feel like Poirot about to reveal the murderer.

'And *that,* ladies and gentlemen, is why, after much soul-searching and meticulous planning, I deliberately arranged for you both to meet here today, at *this* precise moment, and at *this* very table.'

And with those last words ringing in the air I slap my hands on that very table and await the reviews.

Nothing happens straightaway. At first, Frida and Tolly appear to be taking part in one of those mannequin challenges. But then Frida comes alive and starts slow-clapping. It only takes a few claps before Tolly joins her.

Their grudging applause carries on as Frida shakes her head and curls a lip at me.

'And you call yourself a town planner,' she says.

9. THE LONG STORY

After polishing off the last of my chips Tolly decides he needs food of his own. That ends up being some yoghurt, the biggest banana I've ever seen, a bottle of iced tea and a salad roll. He sits down and pushes the chip carton he's been mainly responsible for emptying towards me.

'You should take a leaf out of my book and learn to eat more healthily,' he says.

I don't take the bait. Frida steps in to fill the silence.

'So, Tolly, Sebastian just told me you're looking to do something in Science or Medicine?'

'That's right. Ideally I'd like to get into some kind of scientific or medical research – diseases, stem cells – that sort of thing. Or if I did straight Medicine, one day I'd love to work with someone like Doctors Without Borders.'

'That would be *so* cool.'

I can hear the admiration dripping from Frida's voice. Which I guess is why I respond with this.

'Yes, but Tolly, be careful. What happens when you cure all the diseases and save all the people in those third world and war-torn countries? What happens when your stem cell research means that we live forever? Where's your job security then, eh? Maybe you should seriously reconsider and think about a career in sanitation. After all, as a very wise person once said, "There will always be shit".'

Two pairs of eyes are now trained on me.

Neither pair seems overly impressed with what they're seeing.

'It's what I like to call … humour,' I tell them.

'*Attempt* at humour?' Frida suggests.

'*Failed* attempt at humour,' Tolly concludes.

There is much bobbing of heads then from the two of them before Tolly asks Frida, 'So what about you? What are you thinking of doing?'

'Arts degree, probably with Literature, Creative Writing and Psychology majors. I just love words and stories, creating characters, imagining different lives. That kind of thing.'

Yeah, well, speaking of making stuff up …

'Frida goes to Kingston Girls,' I inform Tolly.

I can tell by the way he looks at me that he's wondering the same thing I did when I first heard that. Perhaps our eye contact lingers a little too long, because it appears Frida has read our shared thoughts.

'Is there a problem with that?'

'No, of course not,' I say. '*Although* … a cousin of mine went to Kingston and I know they're pretty strict and straight there with their uniforms and stuff. Like if your hair ribbon is the wrong shade of green you almost have to appear before a Royal Commission. So I was thinking, you must cop a bit of flak, you know … for your hair and earrings.'

Frida's eyes are boring straight into me.

'Earrings and piercings can be removed, you know. And you might be surprised to learn that when I comb my hair over a bit and tie it back carefully, I can look almost … normal. Maybe even acceptable enough to go to a place like Kingston.'

I really have my doubts about how well that would work, but I can tell she's annoyed so I don't push it.

'Sorry. I wasn't having a go at you. I just didn't think they'd let you get away with anything there, that's all.'

Frida takes her eyes off me and looks down at the table.

'Well, I don't like to talk about it much, but I do have one other thing going for me. It's a bit embarrassing, really, but over the years my parents have donated a truckload of money to the school building fund, and because of that I guess you could say that I'm given a certain … flexibility … when it comes to the rules.'

'Must piss off the other girls a bit?' Tolly suggests.

'Some of them. But that's their problem. I can't help it if I have wealthy and generous parents.'

I'm sorry, but this has the feel of the kindergarten sandpit to me. None of it is ringing true. I know I should probably just leave it, but I can't help myself.

'That would be your father the psychiatrist and your mother the … painter?'

'That is correct,' Frida says deliberately. 'My father, the highly respected and in-demand psychiatrist, and my mother, the very successful and internationally acclaimed painter.'

'Wow. Your mum sounds pretty amazing. Would I know her?'

'You?' Frida replies with a patronising smile. 'I doubt it. She has pretty normal-looking eyebrows.'

Tolly immediately sniffs the air and checks behind my chair.

'Is that you, Sebastian? I thought I smelled someone burning.'

I decide it might be a wise time to retire as question-asker at that point. Frida immediately takes up the baton.

'Anyway, what about Tolly? He's got a bit of a beard thing going on there. I wouldn't think they'd be overjoyed with that at St Jerome's. What's your secret? How do you get away with it?'

Tolly strokes the black hairs above his lip and the thicker growth patches on his chin and jawline.

'It's all in the timing,' he says mysteriously.

Which is true. Every Monday at school Tolly arrives with a freshly shaved face. By Wednesday or Thursday he is usually spoken to for the first time by our homeroom teacher and possibly another class teacher or two about the need to 'get rid of that'. Friday regularly consists of Tolly fielding irritated, 'I thought I told you'-type comments, and him apologising sincerely about his forgetfulness.

That of course leaves Tolly free on the weekend to enjoy his carefully nurtured and treasured facial hair at leisure until the whole process begins again on Monday. Of course now that we're in the middle of our two-week spring break, Tolly's facial growth is significantly more luxuriant than usual.

But Frida seems happy enough just with Tolly's vague answer and moves on to a new topic.

'And what about your name? Where does that come from? Like I told Sebastian, I've never met a Tolly before.'

'Just a nickname,' he tells her. 'You're named after the famous exotic artist. I happen to be named after the famous rabbit dwelling.'

She thinks about it for a moment.

'Warren? Your name is Warren?'

'It's Rabbit Dwelling, actually,' Tolly says matter-of-factly.

Frida giggles, revealing again the slightly crooked teeth that somehow seem to suit her.

'Yes, it's Warren,' he concedes.

'No offence, but I think I like Tolly better.'

'Oh, I'm definitely offended, even though I agree with you.'

'So where does Tolly come from? Is it short for your surname or something?'

'Surname's Pearce. So that would be a no.'

'Where does it come from, then?'

Tolly and I exchange a smile.

'It's a long story,' we say in unison. Then we bump our fists together and do an exploding hands thing along with relevant sound effects.

Frida looks freaked out.

'What was *that* all about?'

'Sorry. Bit of an in-joke,' I explain. 'The thing is, nobody knows where the name Tolly comes from. Except us.'

'Right. And I suppose you can't tell me, because if you did, you'd have to kill me. Is that it?'

Tolly looks impressed.

'You're familiar with our rule book, then?'

I laugh.

Frida doesn't. She's too focused to be distracted.

'So this nickname, did it come about because of some totally obscure thing or would I be able to work it out?'

Tolly and I confer without speaking. He scratches his chin and screws up his face.

'It's *posssssssible* you could work it out.'

'But highly unlikely,' I add.

Frida appears to be weighing this up.

'What do I get if I do? What would my prize be?'

Considering how many people have tried, Tolly and I find this idea a bit amusing.

'What do you get? I don't know. But you'd be really up against it, time-wise. Our drone battle starts in about ten minutes and so does that Drama thing you said you wanted to go to.'

'That's true,' Frida says absently before a smile begins to creep across her face. 'Hey, that's it. That could be my reward for breaking the unbreakable nickname code. Instead of you two going to your stupid drone battles, you have to keep me company at theatre sports.'

'But I thought you were going with friends, anyway?'

Frida hesitates then waves that idea away.

'Well, they're *supposed* to meet me there, but knowing them they'll probably forget or get distracted by something. Or someone. That's if they haven't got bored and gone home already.'

'If that's the case, why don't you ditch the theatre sports and come to the drone battles instead?'

My proposal gets an immediate thumbs up from Tolly.

Frida eyes us both suspiciously.

'Sounds like you guys might be too scared to take me on.'

She's wrong. I'm not scared. I am a bit confused though. I know I'd definitely rather go to the drone battle than to theatre sports, that's for sure. The possibility of being hauled up in front of an audience is my worst nightmare. But the thought of going to theatre sports *with* Frida, compared to going to the drone battles *without* her? That's not so clear-cut to me any more.

'So come on. Are you two prepared to put your drones where your mouths are or not?'

I indicate that I am and wait for Tolly's reaction. He shrugs.

'Sure,' he says. 'And should you succeed in your noble, but almost certainly futile, quest, I will dub thee Frida, the Queen of Cleverdick-ed-ness.'

Frida's eyes light up and she taps her hands together in tiny, rapid claps.

'Ooo, I *want* that title! Now shhhhhh. Don't disturb me.'

For the next five minutes Tolly and I sit silently finishing our lunch and checking our phones while Frida picks at the remains of her sushi and squints down at the table top.

When Tolly catches my attention for about the third time I'm forced to break the silence.

'Um, Frida? We all really should be heading off soon.'

She looks up at me vaguely like she's woken from a dream. Then she retrieves the theatre mask bag from beside her chair and places it on her lap. I feel bad for her. And for me. The stupid in-joke about Tolly's nickname doesn't seem that clever to me any more.

'Time to go,' she says brightly, and pushes back her chair. Tolly and I are doing the same when she stops.

'You know, speaking of *challenges*, it reminds me of this crazy thing I did way back in Grade Eight. It was right at the start of the Christmas holidays, and for some reason I set myself this ridiculous reading challenge to see if I could read the biggest book in the world. And as far as I knew that was ... *War and Peace*.'

Tolly's eyes flash across and engage with mine.

'Have you ever read *War and Peace,* Sebastian?'

I tell her that I haven't.

She rotates slowly to Tolly.

'What about you ... *Warren?*'

He says the same.

'Well, don't worry. It's nothing to be ashamed of, because as you two might say, *War and Peace* is definitely a ... *long story*. Which is exactly why I wanted to read it, just so I could boast that I'd read the biggest book in the world. Silly, I know, but the thing is, I ended up really enjoying it. Weird. Don't you guys think that's weird?'

'Weird,' we both agree.

'And do you want to know another even weirder thing that I've only *just* realised? When you say your name out loud, Tolly, your full and proper name, Warren Pearce, it actually *sounds* a lot like *War and Peace*! Warren Pearce. *War and Peace*. See?'

At this point I am holding my head in my hands. Tolly has slumped back in his seat like a hyper-extended, curly-topped rag doll and is now gazing into the sky with his Adam's apple sticking out like a speed bump.

'Isn't that amazing? Your name, Warren Pearce, sounds like the classic novel *War and Peace* written by ... wait, who was the author, again? Oh, that's right, Leo *Tol*stoy. Good old Leo. Hey, I wonder if Leo ever had a nickname like you do, Tolly, when he was young.'

She pokes a black fingernail into her cheek and twists her mouth to the side in mock concentration.

'Hmmmmmm, now let me think. I wonder what his friends might have called him? What could it possibly have been? *Tols*toy? *Tolllllllll*-stoy? Any ideas, *Tolly*, what *Tols*toy's nickname might have been?'

Tolly has his hands in the air at this point, like he's had enough and is handing himself in. Meanwhile Frida smiles smugly and holds her two small fists above the table.

'Time to bring it home, boys,' she says.

Reluctantly Tolly and I each bump a fist with her and make half-hearted explosion sounds. Frida's are much louder.

'Oooh, it's like the New Year's Eve fireworks!' she squeals. Then she twists her head to the side and smiles sweetly at Tolly. 'Warren? Are you forgetting something?'

'Huh? Oh certainly not,' Tolly says, grinding out the words along with a fixed smile.

He picks up an unused plastic knife from the table and taps it first on Frida's right shoulder and then on her left.

'I hereby dub thee Frida, the Queen of Cleverdick-ed-ness.'

'Right, then,' Frida says, springing to her feet. 'Now hands up which of my loyal subjects sitting around this table are super keen for some theatre sports fun?'

Tolly and I each push a reluctant hand to half mast.

Neither of us is smiling.

Not on the outside, anyway.

10. THE HEAD EXECUTIONER

The theatre sports activity is being held in a small drama space called the Shoebox. It holds around a hundred or so people and is basically just a stage area with wooden tiered seating on three sides.

By the time we arrive it's about three-quarters full. I ask Frida if she can see any of her friends. She has a quick look around. Apparently not. She doesn't appear overly surprised or disappointed by this. Nor does she bother trying to text them. We find some space on one of the side sections. We're two rows from the front. I'm not happy about it.

The members of the Comedy and Improv Club are doing last-minute prop-sorting while the room bubbles away with excited talk and laughter. Over to my right I notice three girls by the entrance scanning the crowd. I turn to Frida. She's sitting forward with her eyes glued to the stage.

'Hey, are they your friends over there?'

She doesn't respond. There's a fair bit of noise around us, so I lean a little closer to the multiple piercings of her right ear and ask again. I get the same non-response. It's not until I touch her lightly on the arm that she turns quickly my way looking worried. I repeat my question a third time and point at the girls still huddled near the entrance.

'Your friends?' I ask again.

She frowns a little then looks where I'm indicating.

'My friends? No.' Then she taps her lobe. 'Sorry. Bad ear.'

I'm not sure if she's being serious or making some kind of a joke about all her piercings, but there's no time to find out, because a short, bouncy girl with blue-tinged hair and a microphone leaps onto the stage and welcomes us all to the Shoebox Theatre. The noise level around the room immediately drops as my stress level simultaneously blasts off in the opposite direction.

There are the two words I'm desperately hoping no one utters while we're here. Audience participation. More like audience humiliation is the way I see it. Why couldn't we have gone to the drones? I'm missing them already. Drones are great. Drones do their thing in the sky. Alone. Drones never expect you to get up there and join them. Drones don't force you to be part of their show. Drones don't expect anything of you at all. They just let you be. People should be more like drones!

Luckily, for the first part of the show I'm safe. It just consists of two university theatre sports teams competing against each other to improvise various weird scenarios thrown at them by the blue-haired girl and members of the audience. It even ends up being good fun. Especially because none of it involves me.

After that wraps up, the MC sweeps a hand around the audience like a searchlight and says, 'Now it's time for some … audience participation!'

Shit. What did I say about no one uttering those two words? But I might be safe. The MC calls for volunteers. I look around. I see hands. Plenty of them. Thank you, insane, confident people! My stomach uncoils as ten volunteers are selected and put through more improv scenarios. When it's over they get a well-deserved round of applause.

So far, so pretty good.

Next a desk is placed on centre stage with a big office chair behind it and a small stool in front of it. The MC holds up a folder and waves it about.

'Time for *The Mystery Job Interview*. I will be playing the role of the interviewer, at least to begin with, and I will be looking for suitable applicants for some pretty *interesting* jobs. The twist is that applicants won't know what job they are applying for until they sit down for the interview. All we need is our first brave applicant to get the ball rolling.'

A number of hands shoot up. Thanks again, you magnificent lunatics! Time to sit back and enjoy the show.

Except the MC has other ideas.

'Sorry. Not taking volunteers for this one. The power and pleasure of selecting an applicant from among your beaming faces is entirely in my hands.' She's now rubbing those hands together like an evil mastermind as she surveys the stands. 'Now, let me seeeeeeeee.'

She's not really an evil mastermind, of course, but she might as well be, because she's scaring the hell out of me. A nervous buzz rises from the audience. The MC's eyes prowl about the crowd until they make their way to our stand and hover around where Tolly, Frida and I are sitting. Shit. I've stopped breathing and I'm doing my best to turn myself into a human chameleon. I don't think it's working. I feel about as obvious as an elephant in a fish tank. And almost as comfortable.

My eyes bore into the back of the person in front of me. I remain motionless and welded to the spot. People are drawn to movement. It's the hunting instinct. I read that somewhere, and there's no doubt that the blue-haired MC is a deadly predator. It's a good plan. Or is it? What if I'm being *too* still? What if my weirdly unnatural lack of movement actually makes me stand out more, like a stationary sore thumb?

My eyes flick up. The MC is smiling. She looks like a sadist. Scrap that. She *is* a sadist! My blood might be running cold but I'm convinced that someone has started a raging fire right under my face.

'How about … *you*?' the sadistic MC asks.

My heart jolts. She's pointing my way. But not at me exactly. More beside me.

Frida places a hand on her chest.

'Yes, my gorgeous girl. Let's see if we can find a job that's just right for you.'

Frida grimaces but stands up. The rest of the audience applaud as she makes her way onto the stage. I exhale a wind farm of tension and try to convince my body to relax.

'And what's your name?'

Frida glances back at me with a sly smile. 'Elsa,' she says.

A light-hearted murmur runs around the crowd.

'Well, anything is possible in theatre sports,' the MC replies, 'so I'm just going to have to … *let that go*. Just hope it's not too warm for you in here, Elsa.'

More light-heated murmuring with a dash of good-natured groaning.

'Thank you so much for that show of support,' the MC tells the audience as she takes up her position behind the desk. 'So,

Elsa, welcome to your *Mystery Job Interview*. Please do come in and have a seat.'

Frida does just that and slips straight into the role of expectant job applicant by squeezing her hands together on her lap and smiling excitedly but nervously back across the desk. The MC runs her eyes over a sheet of paper that we've been told contains a list of highly unlikely positions vacant. When she finds one she likes she carefully lays the sheet back down on the desk and pats it flat.

'Now, *Elsa,* I see here that you are applying for the position of … Head Executioner.'

The audience laughs then bubbles away for a few seconds. The MC continues when they settle.

'Job description – removal of offending heads on demand. No experience necessary. Uniform provided.'

More scattered laughter.

Frida slides enthusiastically to the edge of her seat in anticipation.

'Yes, that's right. It's been my dream job ever since I was a little girl,' she says in her broken, ragged-at-the-edges voice. 'I used to *love* pulling the heads off my Lego figures.'

A good level of chuckles from around the stands.

'Well, that sounds promising, but Head Executioner is a big step up from Lego dismemberment. So what really appeals to you about this particular position?'

Frida makes a big show of giving the question serious consideration.

'Well, there's the free uniform, of course. That's a big thing because I'm sure there's going to be a lot of washing and dry cleaning involved. But, um, the main reason that the position of Head Executioner is so exciting for me is because I think the job itself is just so … cutting edge.'

The crowd love that one.

'Right, and how does your family in general feel about your career choice?'

'Oh, they couldn't be happier or prouder. See, my father's a lumberjack and my mother is … ah … a mortician. So they think Head Executioner is the best of both worlds!'

That gets a solid laugh too and a smatter of applause as well.

'Excellent,' the MC says. 'But I must warn you, Elsa, that we've had a lot of applicants for this particular position, so I'd like you to give three good reasons why you think *you'd* be the best person for this job.'

Frida wrinkles up her nose and inverts her smile into a sad emoji. '*Three* good reasons?'

'Okay, because you've been such a great sport, I'll settle for two good reasons and one pathetic one.'

'Great. No worries. Three reasons why I think I'm the best person for the Head Executioner's job. Right.'

She begins to count them out on her fingers.

'One. Um … I have my own axe.'

A chuckle or two.

'Two. Ah … Black hoodies really suit me.'

A few more supportive laughs.

'And three. Aaaaaaaaah … I love meeting new people – but only for a little while!'

Biggest laugh yet. As Head Executioner, Frida is killing it.

'Outstanding,' the MC says. 'But now I need to know if you have any faults or weaknesses with regard to the job? Be honest, now.'

Frida twists up her mouth.

'Well … I'm not too keen on blood. But don't worry, I'll just take aim, close my eyes and hope for the best!'

She crosses her fingers and beams out a smile that is so cheesy I have to stop myself from doing the same smile right back at her.

The MC shakes her head. 'Well, I'm afraid that *might* …'

Frida's dopey smile vanishes.

'Oh, and some people say I have a really bad habit of interrupting them while they're speaking. But that wouldn't be too much of a problem with this job, would it? You know … *cutting people off*?'

A good-humoured moan erupts from the stands. The MC interlocks her fingers and rests her hands on the application sheet.

'Well, I don't think we can take the risk of any more atrocious puns like that one, so on that note we will conclude our interview. Elsa, you have been an outstanding candidate and I'm happy to say that the job is yours. Very well done!'

Frida receives a big round of applause and some cheers as well. She rises to leave but is immediately halted by the MC.

'Oh, no. We're not quite done with you yet. For being so excellent *you* now get promoted to the interviewer position and have the power to nominate the next applicant.'

Frida might be pretending to be Elsa, but right now I'm the one whose smile is suddenly frozen on his face. Along with every atom in my body. Out on the stage, Frida takes the list of potential jobs from the MC and moves behind the desk. She surveys it and then the audience. I become intensely interested in my hands. It feels like my chest is being squeezed in some kind of giant vice. What are those three signs of a heart attack we learned about in PE, again? I'm pretty sure that I'm rocking at least two of them right now.

Even though my neck feels like it's fused in place, I force myself to look up. Frida is lifting a hand to point. It's the one with the black fingernails. I take this as a bad omen. Her cold, Head Executioner eyes are on me as if she's lining up my neck for her blade.

No way can I do what she's just done so easily. I can't make up stories on the spot out of nothing. I can't just click my fingers and be someone else. Hell, I have enough trouble just being me! And that's the *me* whose mind would shut down the second I set foot on that stage. The *me* who would die out there. And what an excruciatingly painful death it would be. For everyone. I close my eyes and await my fate as a new mantra starts drumming in my head. *Don't pick me. Don't pick me. For god's sake, don't let her pick me!*

'I pick *you*,' I hear Frida say. I'm about to see if my jelly legs are even capable of getting me upright when she adds, 'You with the curly black hair and struggling goatee.'

Beside me Tolly sucks air in through his teeth and winces like he's been struck by an arrow.

The audience claps encouragingly at the lanky figure making his way into the spotlight, especially those like me who are overjoyed that they're not the ones taking that walk of death. I join in the applause and try to slow my breathing and heart rate down to something approaching non-critical levels. Tolly meanwhile strides across the stage and stands, with his arms folded, beside the MC, totally dwarfing her.

'I'm shrinking! I'm shrinking!' she cries as she flaps her arms about and drops to her knees. Her effort is rewarded with some laughter. Not so much from Tolly, whose flat, static smile says that he's seen and heard it all before.

'Right. Sorry about that,' the MC says. 'No weather jokes, I promise. And your name is?'

'Tolly.'

'Tally?'

Laughter.

'*Toll*-y.'

'Right. Interesting name.'

'It's a long story,' Tolly says with a straight face.

At the desk behind them Frida smiles and nods her approval.

'As are you,' the MC says. 'But we're nearly out of time, so sadly we'll have to save that particular story for another day. Okay, *Tolly*. You're our next contender for a *Mystery Job Interview*. Have a seat. Elsa, he's all yours!'

The MC moves away and sits on the edge of the stage while Tolly takes his place on the stool. He makes it look like a piece of kindergarten furniture. His knees are higher than his hips. The audience finds this highly amusing.

Behind the desk Frida runs her eyes up and down the positions vacant sheet before placing it on the desk and drumming her fingers on top of it.

'Welcome to your job interview, Mr Tolly,' she says pleasantly. 'So, tell me, exactly why *have* you applied for the role of Dopey in the stage production of *Snow White and the Seven Dwarfs*?'

Biggest laugh yet.

11. THE BIG LEBOWSKI

The theatre sports presentation wraps up with the three sections of the stands locked in a rowdy sing-off battle to Monty Python's 'Always Look on the Bright Side of Life'. As we file out, there's a happy rumble of chatter and laughter surrounding us.

Quite a few people congratulate Frida and Tolly on their performances. There's even a couple of high fives. Or in Tolly's case, some higher-than-usual fives. Even though Frida was clearly the star of the session, Tolly got his fair share of laughs. The biggest was when he said he wanted to play one of the seven dwarves so that he could really *stretch* himself as an actor. That got the old Shoebox shaking.

'Now own up,' Frida says as we make it outside and the sun hits our faces, 'wasn't that *so* much better than watching a bunch of boring drones just droning around?'

She could be right, but neither of us is going to admit it.

'Better than I thought, anyway,' is all I give her.

'Fine for *some* people,' Tolly fires back. 'You didn't end up being part of the show.

'Terribly sorry about that,' Frida says happily.

'And you sound so sincere. But why me?' Tolly asks her. 'What did I ever do to you? Aren't you two the ones who've been sandpit buddies ever since you were embryos or something? Why didn't you pick *him*?'

Frida makes a big show of giving me the once-over like she's sizing up a rejected used car.

'Hmmmm. Not sure. I thought about it, but I guess I just took pity on him. After all, town planners aren't known for their spontaneous creativity, are they?'

It's meant as another one of her jokes, but something about her answer gets to me, and I find myself wishing that she *had* picked me so maybe I could have proved her wrong. But that's an enormous 'maybe', so I don't wish very long or bother trying to defend myself.

Tolly checks something on his phone.

'Well, I've got an interview with a Science tutor in about half an hour, so Frida, I think the very least you could do to make up for exposing me to public ridicule is to come with us to the Great Court and see if we can still catch the end of the drones display.'

'Sure,' Frida tells him. 'Never let it be said that when forced to, I wasn't willing to do the absolute least I could do.'

It only takes a few minutes to walk to the Great Court. The name says it all, really. It's a massive, grassy courtyard area dotted with big trees, right in the centre of the campus. Surrounding it are sandstone buildings and a walkway flanked with sandstone columns and arches. It really is pretty great.

Normally it would just be a wide open space with a few benches sprinkled about, but today, for the Future Students program, there are food vans and rows of stalls and tents promoting a whole heap of uni clubs, societies and student services. There's also a local radio station giving away prizes and pumping out music from on top of a double-decker bus. And of course, plenty of people.

Tolly leads us straight to the Engineering Society tent. We're too late for the major drone battles, but all is not lost. A netted-off area for micro-drones is still up and running. The challenge is to fly a tiny drone about as big as your palm through a series of hoops and obstacles in the shortest time possible. It's a dollar a shot, with all the money going to charity.

'Here,' Frida says, holding up a two-dollar coin. 'My shout. I actually do feel a bit bad about you guys missing out on your big drone battle fix. So let's see who's the Drone Master here, shall we?'

Tolly suddenly seems very unsure and hesitant. It's not like him at all. I'm immediately suspicious.

'Look, I'd like to take you up on your offer,' he tells Frida, 'but I don't know if I should.'

'Why not? What's wrong?'

He wraps his arm around my shoulders and pulls me close. Not a good sign.

'Well, it's just that I'm really worried about the effect it might have on our mutual BFF Sebastian here. You see, even though he does his best to hide it, he's pathetically uncoordinated, and mentally he's, well … *slow* … is really the kindest word for it. Plus he has a nasty habit of throwing violent, hysterical tantrums whenever he's comprehensively humiliated and destroyed in any sort of a contest. And *that,* unfortunately, is something that *inevitably* happens *every single time* he comes up against me.'

Right. Of course. Well, he did warn me back at the cafeteria that all the girl-phobia crap I dumped on him wouldn't stand.

I pluck the coin from Frida's hand and jab a finger his way.

'And *that* will not stand either, pal,' I tell him.

'You sure now? I'll give you one chance to back out. But then, once spoken it can't be unspoken,' Tolly reminds me. 'Them's the rules.'

Frida is looking at both of us like we're speaking in tongues.

'It. Will. Not. Stand,' I repeat.

We pay our money and the Ultimate Micro-Drone Challenge begins.

And it ends shortly after when Tolly comprehensively humiliates and destroys me.

'Really bad luck,' he says after his drone touches down gently on the black-and-yellow striped finishing pad while mine is being pored over by two clearly frustrated Engineering students who are struggling to rebuild it from the assorted pieces it has become after somehow hyper-accelerating into the dirt. '*Really* bad luck. If only that ground wasn't there, you would've been fine. It's not easy to avoid a planet.'

Fortunately, Tolly has to leave for his interview appointment, so I don't have to put up with this kind of thing for long.

'Meet you guys back here somewhere?'

I check Frida's reaction first. She seems happy enough with that. I'm glad.

'Sure,' I say. 'Text us when you're done.'

With Tolly gone, Frida and I begin working our way around the various stalls and displays. We eventually come to one run by the university Chinese Society. They're giving out free servings of fried rice. It smells delicious, so we join a queue of people hanging around waiting for the next batch to be ready.

Frida takes the opportunity to ask me a question.

'So tell me. What's it with you and Tolly and the whole "It will not stand" thing?' She shakes a clenched fist and says those last words in a macho-type voice. 'Another one of your in-jokes that you can't tell me about?'

'Nah, nothing like that. It's from a movie. *The Big Lebowski.* Ever seen it?'

'Don't think so.'

'Yeah, well, it's pretty old, I guess. Tolly and I only watched it because of his dad.'

'The movie nut?'

'That's the one. Actually, he's a pretty cool guy, Mr Pearce. Bit weird maybe, but in a good way. Been our family dentist for years. He's great too except he always wants to talk to me about movies and stuff when he's got my gob full of metal pokers and scrapers and a massive saliva-sucking tube.'

Frida holds her stomach.

'Lovely image. Thanks for that. What's the rest of Tolly's family like?'

'Pretty normal. His mum's a librarian and part-time belly-dance instructor. She got arrested not long ago for hitting an anti-refugee protester over the head with his own sign. Made the six o'clock news.'

'Just your average suburban mum, then?'

'Yeah. And then there's Tolly's little sister, Tippy. I think she's eleven now. She likes collecting unicorns. She's also a dirt bike and karate champion. Cute but deadly.'

'Tippy?'

'No idea where that comes from. Not even a nickname.'

'Okay, so what's the story with the movie, then? The *Big* …
whatever.'

'*Lebowski*. It just started one day when I was over at Tolly's
place. His dad made some comment about that movie and when
he found out we didn't know what he was talking about he
was like, "You've never seen *The Big Lebowski*? What are they
teaching in schools these days? The Dude abides, man! This will
not stand. This definitely will not stand!" At the time we didn't
realise he was quoting from the film, but to stop him having a
heart attack or something, we said we'd watch it with him.'

'Any good?'

'Great, actually. But we had to throw Tolly's dad out of the
room because he kept saying all his favourite lines along with
the characters and laughing his head off when something funny
was *about* to happen.'

'And the "It will not stand" thing" is part of the movie?'

'Yeah. It's something the main character, the Dude, says after
some crooks threaten him. Although to be totally accurate, what
he really says is, "This *aggression* will not stand, man". For some
reason it just sort of stuck in our heads and Tolly and I started
saying it too, whenever something happened that we couldn't
let go unchallenged.'

I can see Frida's joining the dots together in her mind.

'Like you telling Tolly he had girl problems and then him
saying he always destroys you in contests.'

'Yep, exactly like that.'

'So basically it's just a comeback you guys use when you're

giving each other a hard time,' Frida says, dismissing the whole thing with a pout of her lips and a flick of her hand.

'Yeah. Mostly. But sometimes it can be a *bit* more than just that.'

'More? Like what?'

'I don't know. It's not important. It's just that sometimes it's about other things, that's all. Not just us having a go at each other.'

'What do you mean? What *other* things?'

You'd think I would have learnt by now that you can't make a casual comment around Frida without having to explain it fully and in detail.

'Well, like last year, for instance. We had this new Grade Eight boarder join our tutor group. He came from some little outback country town somewhere and he was having a hard time fitting in. Anyway, one day Tolly and I were talking about him and how miserable he always looked and I can't even remember who it actually was, but one of us just happened to say, "This will not stand." And once we said that, it was sort of like maybe we should actually try to do something. Not just talk about it.'

Frida holds up a finger.

'Once spoken it can't be unspoken,' she quotes.

'Exactly.'

'So what *did* you do?'

'Not that much really. Just simple stuff. Made sure we talked to him every morning in tutor group and at lunchtime when we could. Tried to find out what was worrying him. Got some other Grade Eights who we knew were good kids to include him in their group. Stuff like that. Seemed to work okay. He's fine now. Hard to shut him up, actually. I think we created a monster.'

Frida is staring me. Did I say something wrong? Have I done another mono-brow thing?

'You call that not much? You're goddam superheroes. Got any other "It will not stand" moments like that one?'

'A few but they're not really that ...'

'Tell me.'

'Why do you ...'

'Tell me.'

She's like a pit bull with a bone. She's not letting go.

'Okay. All right. The swimming carnival was another one.'

She's looking at me as if to say, 'Why in the world have you stopped talking?' I have no choice but to go on.

'So, Tolly and I are both in Gold House at school and every year Gold House comes last in the swimming carnival. By about the length of a dozen olympic pools usually. Pretty depressing. Anyway, this year Tolly reckoned *that* wouldn't stand, and I agreed. So because everyone gets a point just for being in a race no matter where they finish, we started a campaign along with the sports captains to really boost our participation rate. You know, stack every race with as many Gold swimmers as we could, even if they came last or couldn't make it to the end of the pool. It didn't matter. As long as they hit the water and didn't drown that was a point for us. Some lower divisions ended up only having Gold competitors on the blocks.'

'And?'

'At the end of the carnival Gold House had powered into *second*-last place by a massive three points.'

'Winning! So what else couldn't stand?'

It doesn't look like she'll ever be satisfied, so I try to overload her a bit and avoid the details.

'Geez, I don't know … Ah, Tolly not being able to swim twenty-five metres in any stroke without drowning. Umm … The pathetic amount of money our tutor group looked like it was going to collect for a cyclone relief appeal. Tolly's sister thinking she wasn't awesome. Some stupid stuff some kids at school were saying about the Muslim boys.'

'What? And you guys fixed all that?'

'No way. We just did something or said something, that's all. Sometimes it helped. But other times it made no difference at all.' A few examples float through my mind.

'Like with Tolly and the gay thing,' I add, without really thinking.

Frida immediately looks up at me. Her dark eyebrows are curved like the tops of two question marks.

'Tolly and the gay thing?' she repeats.

She has that pit bull look on her face again and it's obvious that I'm going to have to tell her the whole story now.

And here's something else that's obvious. At least to me.

My superhero status is about to be flushed down the drain.

12. THE SIDEKICK

The new batch of fried rice has now been stirred and tossed around on the solar cooker and is ready to be served. When we get ours Frida insists we find a place where she can hear all about Tolly and the gay thing in comfort. Great. At least one of us will be.

'So?' she says once we've claimed a shady spot under a big jacaranda tree. 'Tell me about Tolly and the gay thing?'

I take a deep breath and prepare myself to come a distant second-best to Tolly yet again.

'It was last year. One of the Grade Twelves at our school wanted to bring a male partner to the senior formal but our principal said no and he wouldn't budge. It caused a bit of a shit-storm. Even made the paper.'

'So it should. How stupid,' Frida chimes in.

'Yeah, well, that became a big "It will not stand" thing for Tolly, so he started a campaign to try to get the decision changed. First he went to see the principal himself, and when that didn't work, he got people to sign petitions and he put up posters around the school and even sent emails to the Parents and Friends Association and the Old Boys Network asking for support. He got plenty too. But it didn't make any difference. The principal still said no.'

Frida scoops up some fried rice with her fork and pauses before placing it in her mouth.

'And that was the end of it?'

'Not quite. Before school on the day of the formal, Tolly set himself up in the middle of the playground. He was wearing a rainbow-coloured tie-dyed T-shirt and a big sign around his neck that said "St Jerome's Unfair to Gays". When the bell rang for homeroom, he refused to come to class. Our principal was pretty pissed off but Tolly stayed out there until the school called his parents and they convinced him to come in. So he definitely didn't let it stand, but in the end nothing changed. Except maybe Tolly's attendance record and his chances of becoming school captain, because he got a week's suspension.'

A cheap plastic fork is poked my way.

'Don't you tell me Tolly's no superhero.'

I go back to eating for a while but I can feel Frida's eyes still lingering on me. And I'm pretty certain I know the question she's pondering. I wait to see if she'll put it into words.

'But what about you? You didn't join Tolly in the protest?'

Yep. There it is, folks.

'I helped him with the petitions and the posters and stuff but no, I didn't do the protest in the playground with him.'

Frida doesn't react or say anything, but I know she's waiting for me to say more. To explain. Fully and in detail. I also know that there isn't any answer I can give that will save my superhero standing, so I don't bother trying very hard.

'I did ask if he wanted me to do it with him, but he told me not to worry. He reckoned he could make the point just as well by himself and there was no use both of us getting into trouble. He said that his parents would handle it much better than mine. We both knew that was a no-brainer. So yeah. I guess you could say that he talked me out of it. But he didn't have to work very hard. Tolly's not just smarter than me. He's a lot braver as well.'

Stuff it. I've come this far. Why stop now?

'Tolly's a lot more everything than me.'

Frida smiles a little at that as she rounds up the last of her rice grains.

'Don't be too hard on yourself,' she says. 'Not everyone's cut out to be Batman, you know. Someone has to be Robin. Nothing wrong with being a sidekick.'

She drops her fork inside her empty container.

'Basically, as long as you're not one of the arsehole bad guys I think you're doing okay. There's too many of them already. Sidekick beats arsehole bad guy every day of the week in my comic book.'

I'm not sure if she really means any of that or she's just saying it to make me feel better, but the mention of bad guys reminds me of something from back at theatre sports.

'Hey, what did you mean when you said that thing about your "bad ear" before?'

She loops her hair back behind her left ear. And taps it with her finger.

'*Good* ear.'

Then she turns her head so I can see her other ear, the one carrying all the heavy metal, and taps that.

'*Bad* ear.'

It must be pretty obvious that I'm not quite with her, because she repeats the pointing routine with further explanation for me.

'Okay. So *this* one hears perfectly. But *this* one hears not at all.

You were sitting on my bad side. Normally it's not too much of a problem, but in a noisy place like that with everyone talking around me, if you're sitting on the wrong side and speaking close to my bad ear, you might as well be talking to my foot and expecting an answer.'

'Sorry. I didn't realise.'

'Not your fault. Most people don't know about it. I'm pretty good at hiding it. I usually avoid noisy places if I can and I try to stand or sit so most people are on my left.' Then she pats the bag beside her. 'Sometimes I'm so devious that I place stuff on my bad side, which forces the other person to sit on my good side.'

And suddenly something else makes sense to me.

'That's why you swapped seats at the movies. It wasn't to get a better view. I was on your bad side.'

'Sprung.'

'So how …'

'… did it happen?'

'Sorry, I didn't mean to … You don't have …'

'Stop apologising. It's no big deal. Got a perforated eardrum when I was ten. Which just basically means a big hole was blown in it. Then water got into the inner ear and it became badly infected, and because it wasn't treated soon enough, all the nerves were damaged and destroyed. End result. One dud ear. So now I have a division of labour. One ear for hearing. One ear for jewellery wearing. So let's see if you've been paying attention. Which ear do you have to avoid if you want to guarantee you'll be heard?'

I point at the one carrying all the metal.

'Your "bad" ear.'

'She's not *really* bad,' Frida says in the voice of a kindly school teacher. 'She just doesn't *listen*.'

I award that with a forced smile and a shake of my head.

'How do you perforate an eardrum, anyway?'

'Why? Are you keen to try it?'

'Not right now. But curious in case I ever feel the need to.'

'Well, as I found out from the doctor, it's not as hard as you'd think. There's actually a variety of effective methods you might employ for excellent results. You could insert any number of sharp or pointy objects way too far into your ear canal or if you're really lazy, get someone else to do it for you. Alternatively, you could have someone or something whack you very hard right over your ear so that it causes a rapid build-up of air pressure, which ruptures the drum.'

I'm not sure if I should ask the obvious question in my head. But I do.

'So what happened with you?'

She places a hand on her bad ear and runs her fingers over the piercings and the little hanging moons as she drifts into the memory of it. I wait for her to return. She looks up and smiles.

'Tennis,' she says.

It's not at all what I'm expecting. She doesn't really strike me as the sporty type. I try to picture her on a tennis court, but something about the slightness of her arms and body and fairness of her skin make it difficult.

'Yeah, I was playing doubles and I was up at the net. My best friend was behind me on the baseline. She mishit a ball.

Hard. Silly me turned my head just at the wrong time and it got me flush on the ear. Probably a one in a million chance. Bang. Perforated eardrum. And the rest, as they say, is silence.'

'What a bugger. Must be hard.'

'More frustrating. And sometimes embarrassing. I have a problem working out where sounds and voices are coming from. If someone calls out to me I usually look the wrong way. I really miss being able to hear music in stereo too. Earphones don't do much for me any more.'

She rotates her empty fried rice container slowly as some of the humour drains from her face.

'Scares me a bit too sometimes if I'm honest. You know, now that I'm down one ear, what if something goes wrong with the other one?'

She brings the conversation abruptly to an end by holding out her hand for my fork and empty carton.

'But there are worse things that can happen to you in life. Here, give me those.'

I hand them over and she takes them across to a rubbish bin. When she turns to come back, the full sun washes over her face. She closes her eyes and opens her mouth slightly like she's drinking in the warmth. When she gets to me, she frowns.

'What are you grinning at?'

The question surprises me because I didn't realise I was. I'm still trying to come up with an answer when something behind me obviously catches her eye and her own smile makes a comeback.

'What is it?' I ask her.

She grabs her bag with one hand and my wrist with the other.

'It's your time to shine, Robin,' she says, and pulls me to my feet.

13. THE GUITAR

I'm being dragged towards a banner stretched between two trees. The words *Acoustic Society* are painted on it in musical notes. A girl and a guy are seated at a small table beneath it. Scattered behind them are guitars, ukuleles, tambourines and other more unusual musical instruments.

I resist Frida's effort to lead me further.

'Wait. What are you doing?'

She reacts as if it should be obvious.

'You said you wouldn't sing me one of your songs unless you had a guitar. They've got guitars. We can borrow one.'

When she attempts to get me moving again, I hold my ground.

'No. I think you'll find that what I *actually* said was that I *wouldn't* sing you one of my songs even if I *had* a guitar.'

She dismisses my objection with another one of her hand flicks.

'I beg to differ, and given your warped recollection of our first meeting in the sandpit, I'd hardly call your memory … reliable.'

'Well, now *I* beg to differ. And given that our first meeting in the sandpit never even happened, what does that make *your* memory?'

'Okay, so what are you saying?'

'I'm saying that you can borrow all the guitars in the world if you want, but you can't make me play any of them.'

Frida releases her grip on my wrist and positions herself directly in front of me with folded arms. Her mouth is skewed to one side.

'So looks like I was right, then.'

'About what?'

'About not picking you for that theatre sports challenge. Even if you had the ability to do it, you still would have needed the courage. Can't see much evidence of that at present.'

Now I'm getting annoyed. It's perfectly clear what she's doing, and there's no way I want to let her manipulate me like I'm some little kid. But I also want to prove her wrong. I'm trying to figure out how to do that when the taunting expression on her face eases. She wrinkles her nose, which makes the faint white line of the scar on it a little more visible.

'Why write them if no one ever gets to hear them?'

'*I* hear them.'

'And that's always going to be enough for you, is it?'

I'm really not sure what the answer to that question is. When I don't come back with a reply straightaway, Frida leaves me and continues alone to the Acoustic Society desk. A lot of talking, nodding and smiling take place when she gets there. Also pointing. By Frida. At me. Then there's a bit more talking, nodding and smiling before the girl at the desk reaches behind her and picks up a cream-coloured guitar. She hands it to Frida along with a pamphlet. A few seconds later Frida is back. She's standing in front of me, hugging the guitar to her chest.

When I don't react or say anything, she adjusts the guitar strap awkwardly over her neck and begins strumming the strings with a clumsy, flapping hand and a stupid grin on her face. I let her go on for a while before I respond.

'It's upside down,' I tell her.

She stops both her strumming and her grinning.

'What?'

'The guitar. It's upside down. You're playing it left-handed, but it's strung to be played right-handed. So the way you're holding it and playing it, the strings are actually in reverse order to what they should be. You've got the high E at the top rather than the low E. And see this scratch board here? Well, that should be down there. Which it would be if you were holding the guitar right-handed, as you should be, because it's a right-handed guitar. But of course, you're not.'

She looks down at the strings and the scratch board then back at me. She squishes up one side of her face.

'And what, you think I don't *know* that?'

'No,' I inform her. 'I *know* you don't know that.'

She holds her defiant, squished-up expression for a couple more seconds before tossing it overboard like a ridiculously undersized fish.

'Fine. Then why don't you show me how it's done?'

No way. Nah. I'm not falling for that pathetically cheap trick.

'Pleeeease?' she says. 'You wouldn't disappoint a girl, would you? Not on her birthday?'

'It's your birthday?'

She pulls back and looks at me like I'm an idiot.

'No, of course not. But that's what I told them,' she says, indicating the Acoustic Society couple with a tip of her head. 'I said it was my birthday and you were my best friend and you'd written a song just for me but you were a bit shy about playing it.'

I look over at the Acoustic Society information desk. Two sets of eyes are glued on us.

'Oh, and I might also have said that my parents were splitting up and I was flying out to live with my actor mother in LA and this might be the last chance I'd ever have to hear you play the song live before I leave.'

'And they actually *believed* that?'

'Sure. I can be very convincing. The girl on the desk, Jasmine, thought you were so sweet and she said she wished she had a friend just like you.'

I just shake my head as Frida searches for something in her carry bag.

'She also gave me this pamphlet to give to you. Said to tell you that they're always on the lookout for new songwriting blood, and to make sure you join up with them if you get to uni.'

I take the pamphlet and glance back over to the Acoustic Society table again. Jasmine gives a quick wave. I feel embarrassed and guilty, but I wave back and make a big show of folding up the pamphlet and sliding it in my pocket. Frida leans forward and presses the guitar against my chest.

'Pretty please,' she says, peering into my eyes. 'Can't you find it in your heart to grant me this one final birthday wish before we're torn apart by cruel fate?'

I feel like I've been trapped in some sort of a theatre sports challenge, and now I'm being forced to play to a rapt audience of two. I'm not happy about it, but I take the guitar from her without speaking. She turns and gives Jasmine and her companion the thumbs up. They break into smiles and silent hand-clapping.

Frida leads me to a quiet spot behind a couple of vans where people are queuing for ice-cream cones and free fairy floss. We sit down cross-legged on the grass facing each other. Thankfully, we're not within easy hearing distance of anyone.

I prop the guitar on my leg and strum and finger-pick a few chords to check if it's in tune. It's almost perfect, but I stall for time by adjusting a couple of the strings anyway. I strum some more chords. It's an old guitar but it has a nice tone. Frida is silent but her wide, expectant eyes tell me that she's keen for me to begin. I don't share any of her enthusiasm.

'I've written a few things. Different kinds of stuff. I don't know which one to play.'

Frida thinks about it, then puts a hand beside her mouth as if she's sharing some secret and whispers to me in her shredded voice.

'Play the one that the town planner wouldn't have the courage to play,' she says.

14. THE SONG

Being the target of yet another town planner dig is more than a bit irritating, but straightaway I know what song she means. What I *don't* know is whether or not I have the courage to play it.

I rest the body of the guitar as comfortably as I can on my right leg and begin to pick out the opening bars. My throat is tight and my fingers move like big clumsy sausages on the strings. I can't see Frida and I don't want to. I stare at a small patch of grass in front of me and try to forget that she's even there.

All I'm thinking about now are individual blades of grass, the feeling of the strings on my fingers, the sound and vibration of the notes, and the words that I'm hoping I can make come out of my mouth.

I finish plucking the notes of a G chord and move to a C. It's now or never. I take a breath. And I'm singing.

Once there was a day I thought we'd found the key
You tuned yourself to me, forgot the past.
Once there was a day when we sang harmony
And made a memory I thought would last.

The words are coming out more breath than sound. But down in the green world, a tiny beetle is working its way along the side of a blade of grass, and as I follow its progress my voice takes on more shape and form. As I begin the chorus it's like I'm listening to someone else.

So what am I supposed to do now that you've gone away?
How am I supposed to feel? What am I supposed to say?
Should I cry more tears or clench my fists in rage?
How am I supposed to breathe? What am I supposed to be?
How am I meant to turn the page?

I'd planned to stop there, but it's come around so quickly that I find myself going on through two more verses until I'm singing the chorus for the final time. The bug I've been staring at has shuffled to the underside of the blade and now just two of its tiny feet remain visible. I strum the last chord, wait a second, then rest my hand across the strings to deaden them.

It takes a while for the rest of the world to reappear. The world where Frida has been sitting an arm's length away listening to a song and words that I thought no one but me would ever hear. It requires a real physical effort, but I force myself to look at her. She's staring at the same patch of grass I was. She doesn't speak. The silence grinds on for too long and I have to put an end to it.

'So. Probably should just stick to Town Planning then, eh?'

There's another long grind before a single word drops from her lips.

'Maybe …'

Maybe? Who knew that such a tiny, insignificant, nothing kind of a word could hit with such a brutal force? I feel like I've been kicked in the chest and now I'm struggling to breathe as everything inside of me crumbles and falls away.

Frida looks up. A sheen of moisture is in her eyes.

'… but only if you can plan a town that's as beautiful as that song,' she says.

And just like that, someone has reversed the film and I'm gulping in air again and all the bruised and broken things inside of me are being reassembled and rebuilt. Somehow bigger, better and stronger than before.

She's looking down again now, pulling at the grass.

'That song, is it about a real person?'

I tell her it is.

'They must have been important to you.'

I tell her they were and I hope that she will be happy with just that. She's not.

'Some girl, perhaps?'

I'm not sure I can trust myself with words, so I just shake my head.

Frida's eyes are on me now. They don't look like they will be leaving any time soon.

I'm about to speak when my phone buzzes. It's a message from Tolly. I check it, then hold the screen towards Frida. She reads it aloud.

'*Come 2 S7. Level 2. Now!!!* Wow. Three exclamation marks. Wonder what's got him so fired up.'

'No idea, but I think we have to find out.'

'Agreed,' Frida says, standing up and taking the guitar from me. She brushes her fingernails over the strings and smiles. 'You did good, town planner. Now you just have to master my upside down guitar playing technique and there'll be no stopping you.'

She returns the guitar to its owners and when she gets back, we quickly locate S7 on the Open Day app on her phone and head off. There are no more questions about my song.

I'm glad.

15. THE EXPERIMENT

Frida and I stare at the old-fashioned scientific apparatus inside the glass cabinet.

'Pretty incredible, eh, guys?' Tolly says, wedging his way in between us.

Maybe I've missed something here. I take a closer look.

Inside the cabinet is a tall bell-shaped jar. Inside the jar is a glass funnel held in position by a metal tripod. The wide mouth of the funnel contains a black substance. A column of the black stuff fills the narrow section of the funnel and a blob of it is hanging off the end. There are also blobs of the black stuff in a bowl sitting directly below the end of the funnel. The whole thing looks like some kind of weird still-life art installation. There's quite a bit of detailed information on a number of panels behind it, including one entitled *The story so far,* but all I take in is the main heading.

The Pitch Drop Experiment – the world's longest running laboratory experiment.

My mind goes back to Tolly's text and to how excited he was when he met us at the top of the stairs here on level two and how he hurried us over to the display case. I continue to stare at the set-up inside the cabinet for what I consider to be an appropriate period of time before stating what surely must be obvious to everyone.

'Tolly, nothing's happening, man.'

My factual observation jolts him into life. He pushes between me and Frida to get closer to the non-action.

'No, no, no. That's just it. That's the thing. Something *is* happening. You just can't see it!'

He taps a finger on the glass.

'See that black stuff there?' he says, and we both reply in the affirmative because it's impossible not to see it. 'Well, that's pitch.'

'Hey, I wonder if that's why this thing is called *The Pitch Drop Experiment*.'

Tolly ignores my sarcasm and barrels right along.

'Anyway, get this. If you took a hammer and hit that black blob of pitch hanging down, it would shatter and splinter like glass. But here's the amazing thing. That stuff's actually a liquid! It's dripping in big blobby drops through that funnel, only it's doing it so *incredibly* slowly that we can't see it. You'd have to speed up time maybe to something like a year or two per second, and *then* you could see that stuff plopping away like a leaky tap.'

Tolly puts his closed fists up beside his temples, spreads his long fingers out and makes an explosion sound with his mouth.

'Mind officially blown,' he says with a mad grin. 'Don't you see? You think it's one thing, but it's actually something else. Isn't that nuts? It's like a solid *and* a liquid – at the same time!'

Frida and I make brief eye contact. It doesn't seem like she's going to comment, so it's left to me to try to drum up some fake enthusiasm for Tolly's sake.

'Right. Wow. Yeah. Nuts.'

But it's nowhere near enough to satisfy Tolly, because it just sets him off again.

'Look, you really have to read all the stuff at the back of the cabinet to realise how amazing this whole thing is. See what it says there? It's the world's longest running laboratory experiment. The longest one ever. In the world. They started it way back in 1927. Can you believe that? It's in *The Guinness Book of Records* and everything. They set it up to demonstrate the viscosity of tar – you know, how *thick* it is. And guess what? From their calculations they worked out that it's about a hundred billion times more viscous than water. One hundred *billion* times!'

Tolly waits for a suitable response from us. Once again Frida is no help, so I wing it on my own again.

'Phew. One hundred billion times more viscous than water? That's a … heap of viscosity right there. Glad they worked that one out. Handy to know.'

He seems happy enough with that.

'Yeah, and of course it's a really big thing – *huge* – when a drop finally falls off. Only nine have dropped so far. The last one fell back in 2014. And here's another crazy thing. Only four hundred and eighty-three people have ever seen one of the Pitch Drops fall. That was the last one. They had a camera all set up for the previous one but they missed it because of some kind of "technical problem". Can you believe that? Waited all that time, then missed it anyway. Wouldn't that be a killer? Of course, now they've got a live Pitch-Cam on it. See it there? And there's this group who call themselves *The Tenth Watch* who are officially waiting for the next drop. They've got their own Facebook page and you can join them online.'

'And don't tell me, I bet you're going to do just that.'

Tolly shakes his phone excitedly at me.

'Already have!'

Frida raps her long fingernails a couple of times on the glass cabinet. I like the clicking sound they make. It appears that at last she's about to contribute something to the discussion. Tolly and I wait to see what it will be.

'So, what about this one, then? When's number ten due to fall?'

Tolly takes Frida asking him a question as some sort of a major breakthrough, because he becomes even more animated, almost to the point of hyperventilation.

'Well, it's hard to pin down absolutely accurately. You see, the time between drops has been a little inconsistent due to all these variables like vibrations and changes in humidity and air temperature. *Apparently*, after the seventh drop they installed air conditioning in here, which made it colder and slowed everything down even more. But going on past trends and averaging things out, they estimate that the drop hanging there right now will fall in about twelve or fourteen years' time.'

Frida and I stop studying the experiment and study each other instead. I'm guessing that my face looks about as stunned as hers. It's like she's flesh and stone – at the same time!

We confront Tolly together.

'It's due to drop in about *twelve* or *fourteen* years' time,' I repeat to make sure I'd heard correctly.

Tolly's bobbing head excitedly confirms this to be true. Frida bites on the corner of her bottom lip then addresses me.

'Well then, Sebastian, I can *certainly* see why Tolly wanted us to hurry to get here, then, can't you?'

'Sure can,' I reply. 'And lucky he did too. I mean, just think, if we'd dawdled or allowed ourselves to be sidetracked along the way for just say … a bit over a *decade* … we might have missed it completely.'

Frida looks suitably horrified at this prospect.

'Yes, that's right. Oh, and I just thought of something else,' she says, with her eyes stretched wide. 'Remember how when we were leaving the Great Court we passed that girl doing performance poetry, and remember how sensational she was and how I said that I really, *really* wished we could stay and hear more but you said, no, we'd better not, because Tolly's message sounded so *urgent*?'

'Yes. Yes, I do remember that distinctly.'

'Well, I'd hate to think what might have happened if I hadn't listened to you.'

I throw in some appropriate wide-eyed horror of my own.

'Why … we might not have even been here yet.'

Frida's mouth drops open and she sways a little like she's about to faint.

'Oh my god. You're right. And even if we did make it in time, just think of how much of the *twelve* or *fourteen* years of exciting, edge-of-your-seat, lead-up we would have missed.'

'Well, for a start,' I say, pointing at the rigid, knobby and completely-motionless-to-the-naked-eye column of pitch suspended from the end of the glass funnel, 'we would have missed *this* bit right here.'

Frida gasps.

'Unthinkable,' she whispers with a shudder.

'Unforgiveable,' I add.

We wait a second or two then turn round to observe the effects of our performance. Tolly's facial expression and the blob of pitch now have a lot in common. His head swivels from me to Frida then repeats the journey. When neither of us speaks he claps his hands together like he's praying and smiles at us disturbingly.

'So. Are we all done here? Are we all finished? Have we had our little joke? Managed to get all that amusing banter out of our systems now, have we? Please, just tell me if there's more. I wouldn't want the world to miss out on any of your hilariously witty double act.'

Frida and I consult briefly.

'No, I'm pretty happy with that,' I say. 'Unless you …'

'No. No, I'm good,' Frida agrees.

'Lovely,' Tolly gushes. 'Well, now that you've concluded your *très* amusing comedy routine, you might be interested to learn that I urged you to hurry here because I have decided to go to a question and answer session with postgraduate Science students, which is being held next door in lecture theatre A6 at three thirty. That's three thirty by the way, which I'd like to point out is not in twelve or even fourteen years' time, but in about ten minutes, and before I left I wanted the thrill of sharing this iconic piece of science with you. Now, if you two ingrates don't mind, I need to pee. Badly. I think the excitement of witnessing the Pitch Drop Experiment first hand has been a bit too much for me.'

Tolly strides off in the direction of the toilets, which are across the foyer and down the corridor. I don't let him get too far before calling out after him.

'And Tolly, don't worry about this iconic piece of science while you're away. We'll keep our eyes on it in case something happens.'

'Oh, and if you like I'll film it on my phone, so you don't miss anything,' Frida reassures him.

Tolly covers both his ears but manages to leave one finger on each hand sticking up in the air just for us. Frida and I watch him until he elbows his way through the bathroom door and disappears from view.

Then we look at each other and burst out laughing.

Frida smothers her mouth with both hands to stop herself, but it only makes it worse. Her cheeks blotch red and her eyes squeeze into narrow slits that glisten with tears. If it wasn't for the sounds she's making you might think she was weeping in pain. We both struggle to get it together, but then our eyes meet and we lose it all over again.

Our laughter is finally cut off by a sharp voice slicing through it.

'Yo, Casper! Getting *friendly*, again, eh? Always spreading joy, aren't you – and other things? Can't wait to hear all about it back at school.'

A different kind of laughter follows those words. One that is harsh and mocking. I look back over my shoulder. It's coming from down the opposite corridor where a stocky, dark-haired boy stands sneering and grinning. He waves as he joins a line of students filing into a lecture theatre. I don't take my eyes off him until he steps inside.

'Who the hell's that prick, and what's his problem?'

I don't get an answer. When I turn back, I see why. It's not because of Frida's bad ear, which is what I first thought. It's because she's no longer with me. But she isn't too far away. Just across the foyer, in fact.

Yanking a fire extinguisher off the wall.

16. THE FIRE EXTINGUISHER

By the time I make some sense of what's happening, Frida is already on her way to the lecture theatre doors with the canister tightly tucked under one arm and a hand firmly clasped around the nozzle.

'Frida, wait!'

She shows no sign that she's heard me, and I'm pretty sure that's also got nothing to do with her bad ear. I catch up quickly and step in front of her.

'What the hell are you doing?'

She looks in no mood to talk. Her eyes are locked in place and her lips are pressed so hard together they're disappearing into each other. Without answering she steps to the side to go around me. I spread out my arms and block her.

'You shall not pass!'

I'm hoping she'll find my *Lord of the Rings* reference amusing. She doesn't. Not at all. Her eyes are blazing at me now. She steps deliberately the other way. I move to block her once more. She steps back. I block that move as well.

'Get out of my way.'

It carries all the threat and menace of a final warning.

'Look, I can see you're really upset, but can you just stop and calm down for a bit and think about what you're doing? You can't just go around taking fire extinguishers – especially when there's no actual fire. It's … stealing. Not to mention dangerous. What if there *is* a fire and someone needs it? Come on. Please.

Just put it back or you'll get yourself in a heap of trouble. I mean, what exactly were you thinking of doing with it, anyway?'

Her eyes flare and she bares her teeth. It's not a reassuring look.

'What exactly am I thinking of doing with it? *This* exactly. I'm going to go into that lecture theatre behind you and I'm going to find that moronic dickhead who shouted at me just now and I'm going to take this thing here,' she says, holding up the long nozzle and waving it disturbingly close to my nose, 'and I'm going to shove it as far down his stupid throat as I can possibly get it and *then* I'm going to pump that prick so full of whatever shit is inside here until he either chokes to death or explodes. *That's* what I'm going to do. *Exactly*.'

Not quite the answer I was anticipating.

'Right. Okay. It's obvious you have a clear step-by-step plan in mind. So, you know, credit for that. *But* have you really thought this thing through? I mean …'

'Stop talking and just get out of my way.'

I try to look as apologetic as I possibly can.

'I'm sorry. I'd love to, but I can't. I can't let you do it.'

Frida's ragged, teeth-clenched voice comes back at me with unnerving calmness.

'Yes, you can. It's easy. Just step aside.'

'Okay, you're right. Technically, I *can*. But … I'm just not going to. I'm sorry, I'm not letting you go in there and do something stupid that you're gonna regret. I'm not. Jesus, they'll call security on you. Probably the police. If you only do half of what you said, you'll be arrested for assault. At the very least they'll fine you for wilful damage of property or something. Look, I've got no idea what this is all about and why you're so worked up, but if you go in there the way you are now, you'll get yourself into all sorts of shit. And I'm sorry, but I'm not going to let that happen. You need to stop, take some deep breaths and calm down.'

I can see her grip tightening around the fire extinguisher. She doesn't look at all like she's about to follow my advice. I've got a very bad feeling about how all this might play out.

'I am going in there,' she tells me flatly, 'and if you lay a hand on me to stop me, I'll scream this place down and *you'll* be the one who ends up getting arrested.'

Maybe she's bluffing? She *has* to be bluffing. So why doesn't she look like she's bluffing?

I give up trying to second-guess her because it doesn't matter either way. I've gone too far to back down now. I reach out and without making contact with her I clamp my hands around the neck and the base of the extinguisher.

'Whatever,' I say, trying to sound more in control than the churned-up, nervous wreck I feel. '*You* can go in there if you want, but *this* is staying right here with me.'

It's a stand-off. I don't think there's anything she can do. I'm pretty sure that I'm stronger than her. But who knows? She's crackling with anger. I can almost feel it sparking off her and throbbing through the extinguisher that we're both latched on to. It's a raging, Hulk-like anger. And I've seen what that big green guy can do when he's pissed off.

I study her face, trying to anticipate her next move. Red-hot tracer bullets are flying non-stop at me from her eyes. Or they are until she blinks. And blinks again. Now her bottom lip and chin are beginning to twitch and tremble. A single tear, stained with a trace of black make-up, smudges its way down beside her nose. She looks like she's about to shatter.

And I've got absolutely no idea what to do. Or what to say.

'Hey, I thought you guys were supposed to be watching the Pitch Drop for me just in case it falls?'

Tolly is peering down on us. His glasses are on the end of his nose, making his eyes look extra big. Frida screws up her face into one last angry ball and shoves the fire extinguisher hard into my chest.

'Take it,' she says, spitting the words at me. 'You win. Congratulations.'

She spins away and storms across the foyer to a long bench over by the far wall. She flops down on it, closes her eyes and lets her head fall back against the brickwork. Beside me, Tolly sighs and makes a *tsk*ing noise.

'I can't leave you two alone for even a few minutes, can I? When will you ever learn to share your toys and play nicely together?'

I take no notice of his questions and instead fill him in on what's happened. When I've told as much as I know, we go over to where Frida sits as motionless as a marble carving. I push the fire extinguisher under the bench and sit on her good side. Tolly takes the other. Her head is still back and her eyes closed. Tolly nods at me. It's obvious that he thinks it's my job to say something.

'So, Frida … you want to talk about it? You want to tell us who that guy is?'

She releases a long breath, lets her head flop forward and opens her eyes as if she's been pulled out of a trance.

'No. And he's no one.'

'Yeah, that's what I thought,' I tell her. 'Just a random no one you were very keen to kill with fire retardant.'

She pushes a hand through her hair and holds it in a clump on top of her head before she lets it fall.

'Look, he's just some idiot from school, okay?'

I know Tolly will be thinking the same thing as me. Something about how Kingston Girls College must have *really* lowered their entry standards. But it's not the time, so I let it go.

'Well, what's this clown's problem, then?'

'Me, apparently. Likes to call me stupid names. Gets off on spewing offensive and sexist comments at me and spreading foul rumours about my sex life.'

'What an arsehole.'

'Well spotted.'

'So what happens at school with you two? Are all the fire extinguishers locked away or something?'

'At school I ignore him. I don't give a shit about him there. But he's not going to bring his crap here. No way. Not here. Not to this place. It's too important to me. I won't let him. I won't.'

She's squeezing her fists into tight, white-knuckled balls. Dampness is swelling in her eyes again. She brushes the back of her hand roughly across her cheek and notices a smudge of make-up on her fingers.

'Shit.'

She points over at the toilets.

'I need to …'

But before she leaves, Tolly has a question.

'What's his name?'

'Who?'

'Prick Boy.'

'What difference does it make?'

'Just interested, that's all.'

'Why?'

'Because I'm a naturally curious person. Must be my scientific mind. Thirst for knowledge and all that. Come on, humour me. His name?'

Frida hesitates but then her shoulders slump like she's lost the energy to resist.

'Gary Vogel.'

'Gary Vogel?' Tolly repeats, to make sure he has it right.

'You got it,' Frida says, and leaves.

Tolly watches her go. Then he turns to me.

I know the look on his face only too well. And what he's thinking. I also know what the next words to come out of his mouth are going to be. So I save him the trouble and say them for him.

'This will not stand?'

Tolly folds his arms and stares over my head at the doorway through which Gary Vogel disappeared.

'No, young Sebastian,' he says. 'It definitely will not.'

17. THE LECTURE

I have no idea what Tolly has in mind as I follow him across to the lecture theatre entrance.

We both look inside. It's a big space. We're right at the back of the room, and curving rows of padded red and black seats slope down to a stage area with a long bench, a lectern and two massive screens. A few people are still straggling in through the lower entrance but the room is almost full. There must be close to three hundred people waiting for a talk to begin.

'Which one is he?' Tolly asks.

I spot him about halfway down.

'There. Red shirt. Black hair. Mucking around with the guy beside him.'

I watch Tolly's eyes zero in on his target.

'What are we going to do?'

He doesn't answer straightaway but his eyes move from Vogel to the lectern.

'Not we. Me. I got this,' he finally announces, and strides back outside.

Tolly's reading the poster on the noticeboard outside the entrance when I join him. Apparently the talk is by a Professor Anil Bhatt, the head of the Law Faculty. His presentation, which is due to start in a couple of minutes' time, is called Law and Mordor. Catchy title at least.

When he finishes checking out the noticeboard, Tolly selects a few handouts from the table beneath it and makes to leave.

'Hey, wait. Where're you going?'

'Down there,' he says.

He's pointing at a set of stairs leading to the lower level. There's a sign beside them that says, *To Theatre B9 – Front Entrance.*

'Just need to deliver a quick message before I go to that Q and A session. See you in about an hour or so.' And before I get the chance to ask him what he means, he's off.

Now I'm totally lost. What message? What's he on about? I wander back over to the top doors and look inside. I locate Gary Vogel again. He's hard to miss, sprawled in his seat laughing with his mates and making a paper plane from one of his handouts.

'What are you doing?'

It's Frida. She's moved in beside me and is now scanning the packed lecture theatre. Her face hardens when she spots Vogel and his crew. Then something else distracts her.

'What's Tolly doing down there?'

I follow her line of sight. Tolly is by the front entrance. He must have left his bag outside because all he's holding is a computer notebook and a folder.

'Have not got a clue,' I say in answer to her question.

Tolly moves forward but no one really notices him until he steps up onto the rostrum area and begins to stroll across it towards the lectern. And then something truly freaky and bizarre happens. When people do notice him, the noise and chatter in the room start to die away as if he's someone important. Then as other people become aware of the fading noise level, they follow suit and the whole place folds down into silence.

Frida and I swap an 'are you seeing what I'm seeing?' look.

What's going on here? It's just Tolly. Just some high-school kid the same as most of them. But that's not what they're seeing. They're seeing some scraggily bearded giant in an old man's jacket who, if you didn't know any better, could be somewhere in his twenties. Maybe older. By the time he's positioned himself behind the mic, Tolly has become the centre of everyone's attention.

There's no way I'm missing this, so I signal to Frida and we slip inside and sit on the top step of one of the side aisles. Meanwhile, down behind the lectern, Tolly is making everyone wait as long as possible while he mucks around positioning his notebook and shuffling through the contents of his folder. I'm finding it hard not to burst out laughing at all the serious faces trained on him. Only Frida's face has a different expression. One of stunned, and slightly terrified, disbelief.

Finally Tolly is ready. He clears his throat, pushes his glasses back and speaks.

'Before you all have the honour and pleasure of hearing Professor Bhatt speak this afternoon, I just have a few brief but important pieces of information to give you regarding various aspects of the Law Faculty.'

He looks up then and waits an awkward few seconds before he adds with just a hint of impatience and annoyance, 'You *might* want to copy them down.'

Genius.

His suggestion results in a frenzied scratching around for pens, folders, laptops and iPads. Unbelievable. It's like Frida and

I are part of some kind of weird brainwashed cult, but we're the only two who can see through the out-of-control maniac who's leading us.

When the room quietens down again, all Tolly does is read out random information from the handouts everyone there would already have. But it doesn't make any difference. They still copy it down or pretend to, in order to show that they're doing the right thing. It's insane. I mean, who do they think Tolly is, anyway? One of the Law tutors? A postgrad student? President of the campus Law Society? It doesn't really matter much, because whatever Tolly's selling, they're buying. In bulk.

After he's done with the notices, Tolly picks up a slip of paper from his folder, adjusts his glasses and looks down at it.

'Oh, and I have one last message to deliver. It's for a Mr … Gary Vogel.'

From beside me a raspy 'Oh my god' escapes from Frida's lips.

Tolly takes off his glasses, places them carefully on the lectern and surveys the audience.

'Is there a Gary Vogel present today? If so, could you please make yourself known?'

That kills me. 'Make yourself known'. He's stolen that line straight off our school principal. He's killing me.

A bit of murmuring and general gawking around follows. Frida and I know exactly where to gawk. To our left and down about ten rows. That's where Vogel is twisting about in his seat and checking with his mates that he's heard right. Finally he sticks his hand in the air. He doesn't seem too displeased that the focus of the room is now centred on him. But something tells me his attitude might be about to change.

Tolly replaces his glasses.

'Thank you, Mr Vogel. The message I have for you is a very important one, so you would do well to listen carefully. It's this …'

Tolly pauses and lets every trace of warmth and humour drain from his face.

'Don't be a dick your whole life, son.'

Frida's mouth drops open and she grabs my arm with both her hands. No one else knows quite what to do. Some people laugh nervously. Many are looking confused. Some of the parents present look shocked. Did they hear that right? Lots more people are now twisting round in their seats to get a better look at the target of these totally unexpected words. Vogel himself is reacting like he's just had a tub of iced water dumped over him. His face is red and his head is spinning round everywhere trying to make sense out of what's just happened.

But Tolly isn't finished.

'In addition, Mr Vogel, if you are lucky enough to one day undertake Law at this great institution, I strongly advise that you pay close attention to any lectures presented on harassment – sexual and otherwise. In the meantime, that message can serve as a useful summary. I'll repeat it once more for your benefit. Don't. Be. A. Dick.'

There was no mishearing it this time. The whole room is buzzing and bubbling now. Anger, confusion and embarrassment are fighting each other for control of Gary

Vogel's face. But most of the faces turned his way are cold and questioning.

Down at the front of the theatre Tolly acts as if he is totally oblivious to the uproar he's created. He gathers up his folder and notebook, wishes everyone the very best of luck in their upcoming school exams and casually vacates the stage. On the way out he passes an unsuspecting Professor Bhatt coming in. Tolly holds out his hand. Professor Bhatt shakes it. The Professor looks more than a little bewildered by the pandemonium in the room as Tolly makes his exit.

I feel like cheering and giving Tolly a standing ovation but I restrain myself. Frida looks like she's just witnessed the second coming.

'Oh my god,' she says. 'Oh my god. I think I love Tolly.'

I throw up my hands in despair.

'Great. Well, now you know the *real* reason I kept you two apart all these years.'

A crooked smile creeps to her lips. It makes me smile to see it.

18. THE SECURITY GUARD

Frida and I escape the lecture theatre while it's still in a bit of chaos. It takes a few minutes for her to shake herself enough out of her zombie mode to speak.

'What … just happened … in there?'

'Not sure, but I'd say that Vogel guy got well and truly Tollied.'

'Uh-huh,' Frida says, kind of spaced-out and overwhelmed like someone who's just discovered she's in the Matrix. 'You know what? I think I could do with a coffee. You wanna maybe get a coffee? I wanna get a coffee. Let's get a coffee. Yeah, that would be good. Coffee. Let's do that.'

'Okay, but first, how about we get a coffee?' I suggest helpfully.

'Even better idea.'

We're heading for the stairs that lead to the ground floor exit when I remember something.

'Shit. Wait on. I'd better put that fire extinguisher back.'

I jog over, drag the canister out from under the bench where I'd tucked it and take it down the corridor to the empty wall bracket. I'm trying to figure out how to reattach it when a deep voice booms in from behind me.

'Hey! What do you think you are doing with that?'

I spin round with the extinguisher still cradled in my arms. A security guard shaped like a wrecking ball is standing right behind me. He's all I can see. It's like a human eclipse of the Earth. I'm guessing he's either of Maori background or from one of the islands in the South Pacific. Geez, by the size of him, he could even *be* one of the islands in the South Pacific. He doesn't look that old. Maybe early twenties. It's difficult to tell. One thing is clear to me though. The collar and sleeves of the blue shirt he's torturing were never intended for a neck and biceps like his. I'm hoping he's friendly and understanding. If he is, he's hiding it really well. The tattoos snaking up his neck and his shaved head don't help much. He has a badge on his barrel chest. It informs me that I've come face to intimidating face with Tomas Paonga.

'It's okay, mate. I'm not doing anything,' I tell him. 'I'm just putting this back, that's all.'

I feel like a little kid who's been caught shoplifting lollies. It's a pretty safe bet that I look and sound like one as well.

'So you think I'm an idiot, do you?' he says in a voice that chugs along laying down individual words like heavy stone blocks.

But no, I absolutely do not think that he's an idiot and I'm desperate that he doesn't for one second think that I do think that he's an idiot.

'No. No way. I'm telling you the truth. I was just putting it back. Really. Here, you can have it.'

He takes the extinguisher from my hands and shakes it. His top lip appears to have a permanent curl and his dark eyes never leave me. Well, what I can see of them anyway. Again his words start tumbling out in chunky syllables while his expression, which seems to be one of barely restrained hostility, never alters.

'Been spraying it around, eh? Having some fun? Showing off to your mates? To your girlfriend?'

'What? No. I haven't even got a girlfriend. I told you already. I wasn't doing anything with it. I'm just returning it. I am. Really.'

He carries right on throwing down his words and burying me under them.

'Not a toy, you know. Expensive. Important too. Saves lives, eh? What if there was a fire and now it's empty? Or broken. Or missing. Not so funny then, is it? Stealing and damaging university property. That's no joke. That's a crime, eh?'

Crime? This is getting way out of hand.

'Look, just listen, okay? Just listen to what I'm saying. I'm telling the truth. I'm *not* taking it. I *haven't* used it. I *didn't* damage it. I *wasn't* mucking around with it. I was just putting it back. That's all I was doing. Putting the stupid thing back!'

I search for some warmth or sympathy in his small, dark eyes. I don't find it. He reaches down to remove something from the bulky belt that's straining to encircle his waist. It's overloaded with pockets, pouches, and equipment. For a heart-thumping second I think he might be going for a gun. Thankfully he doesn't have one. He extracts a notepad and a pen instead.

'ID.'

'Sorry, what?'

'ID. Student card? Driver's licence? Learner's permit?'

I grab my head to stop it from exploding.

'Are you kidding me? You're kidding me, right? Look … please … this is ridiculous. It really is. I haven't done anything wrong. I haven't done *anything*! I'm telling you the truth. Can't we just …'

'ID,' he repeats, somehow managing to sound even less caring.

I'm dragging out my wallet and still protesting my innocence when I hear a familiar worn-at-the-edges voice.

'He's not in any trouble, is he? Please don't tell me he's in trouble. He was only trying to help. This is all my fault. What is *wrong* with me? I'm such an idiot.'

Frida has stepped from behind the man mountain and is now standing between us. Her face is scrunched up with worry and her dark eyebrows are pushed into an upside down V.

The security guy lowers his notepad and pen.

'And who are you, Miss?'

'Zoe Kahlo.'

I resist the urge to roll my eyes.

'Do you know this boy?'

'Not really. We just met a few minutes ago. Sort of. He was only trying to help me, that's all. If he's in any sort of trouble it's not his fault. If anyone's to blame it's me, not him.'

Frida has Tomas Paonga's attention. And mine. I decide to just keep my mouth shut and let her do what she does best. Make stuff up.

She buries her face briefly in her hands.

'Okay. This is so embarrassing. The thing is, I *thought* there was a fire in the Ladies. The one back there. I opened the door and I saw this big cloud of smoke and I just … panicked. Totally panicked. I called out for help. And he turned up.'

She's pointing at me.

'Sorry, I don't even know your name.'

'Sebastian,' I blurt out before a quick flare-up in Frida's eyes makes me realise that I probably should have come up with something different.

'Hi, I'm Zoe,' she says before continuing with her story. 'Anyway, I told him that the toilets were on fire and he ran and got the fire extinguisher and just charged in. He was only trying to help. But I was wrong. It was a false alarm. *I* was a false alarm.'

Frida twists up her face and rakes a hand through her hair.

'I feel so stupid now. It was just a bunch of schoolgirls puffing away on something in there. Gave them a huge fright. They weren't too happy with me. No need for that sort of language though.'

Tomas Paonga's default expression still hasn't wavered. Frida closes her eyes and lets her shoulders sag. Something tells me that she's about to take it to the next level.

'Look, I know what I did *sounds* stupid, and I guess it *was* stupid, but … ever since our house burned down when I was a little girl, smoke and fires, they just totally freak me out.'

Tomas Paonga is certainly listening now. He's not the only one.

'I'm sorry. I can't help it. It just brings everything back. Being in that room. Waking up with my eyes stinging and my lungs burning. My dad dragging me out. Not knowing if the rest of my family was safe. Losing Nan …'

Losing Nan?

Frida fights to compose herself.

'I've tried to get over it, but nothing seems to work. Any sign of smoke or fire, even in a movie or on the news, still does my head in. Always will, probably.'

Frida raises her eyes to Tomas Paonga's large, impenetrable fortress of a face. It's impossible to tell if her words have had any effect. She reaches for her mobile.

'Look, I don't blame you if you don't believe me. If you want I'll give you our number and you can ring my dad. He's a Senator. Senator Kahlo? Maybe you've heard of him? Anyway, he'll be able to tell you that everything I've said about the fire is true.'

There's a flicker of movement in Tomas's eyes. They shuffle between the two of us. And settle on me.

'This is what happened?' he asks, and I let him know that yes, this is absolutely one hundred per cent what happened.

'So why didn't you say so yourself?'

Excellent question, Tomas! I search my brain for some kind of plausible answer.

'Because … I … just thought … Well, I thought it would sound so *weird* … that you wouldn't believe me … that you'd think it was all, you know, just … made-up bullshit.'

Tomas lays the extended edition of his default expression on me. Then he sniffs and slides his notepad and pen back into the pocket on his belt.

'You were right to think that. Now go. Both of you. Go. But if I have any more trouble from either of you … it will not be good. Do you understand what I am saying to you?'

Clear as a very deep-sounding and slowly tolling bell, Tomas!

Frida and I thank him perhaps a little too much and then get the hell out of there as fast as we can and head for the Great Court. We arrive at the walkway without sharing a word. I'm happy to keep it that way because too much is whirling around in my head. But not Frida.

'You're angry with me, aren't you?'

'What makes you think that?'

'Because you haven't said a word for ages and you're sulking.'

She's right, of course. But I don't tell her that.

'Why would I be?'

'Why? Well, because from what I've seen, you're a pretty straight sort of person who doesn't like doing the wrong thing or getting into trouble and all that stuff back there with the security guy would have really worried and embarrassed you and now you're thinking that none of it would ever have happened if I hadn't been stupid and crazy enough to take that fire extinguisher off the wall in the first place so therefore it's all my fault you got into trouble and that really pisses you off but you're too nice to say anything to my face, so you've decided instead to suffer, and probably curse me repeatedly, in silence. That's why. How did I do?'

I ponder Frida's in-depth analysis before I reply.

'You *sure* you don't want to become a therapist after uni?' I ask her. 'Because I think you'd be a great loss to the profession.'

19. THE KAREN KRATZMAN STORY

We continue along the walkway that circles the Great Court. We're silent again, but I'm all too aware of Frida taking exaggerated glances at me every so often. I ignore her so she finally gives up and speaks.

'*However*,' she says, 'even though I fully understand and sympathise with your current totally-pissed-off-at-me status, I would like to just point out in my defence, that I did *sort of* come to your rescue back there and save you from the security guy with that story I told.'

This is correct too, but it just pisses me off even more.

'Yep, can't argue. You did that, all right. Thanks heaps. You have a rare talent for saying things that aren't true.'

That last bit sounds harsher and nastier said out loud than I imagined in my head. Harsh and nasty enough to make Frida pull up mid-step.

'Whoa,' she says. 'You got something you want to say to me, Sebastian? Something you need to get off your chest?'

I pull up as well.

'Maybe I have,' I tell her.

We've stopped in the middle of the walkway, and because we're about to get trampled by a crowd of students and parents being led by a flag-carrying volunteer on one of the last campus tours of the day, we move between two sandstone columns to a quieter more private spot on the edge of the Great Court.

Once there, Frida faces me and spreads out her arms.

'Well, here I am. Don't hold back.'

I accept her invitation.

'Okay then, you know all the things you said today, the things you told me about yourself? Well, I was just wondering, how much of it is actually true? I mean, you made up all those stories for *other* people – the security guy, Helena, those two from the Acoustic Society – so maybe I'm just like them. How would I know? Maybe everything's like another round of theatre sports to you and I'm just another audience for your stories. Like that stuff you told me about your parents. Is that true? Is your mother really a famous painter or is she a divorced actor now? And what about your dad? What was he again? A psychiatrist? A senator? A lumberjack? It's a bit hard to keep up. And even you. I mean, who am I really talking to here? Frida? Elsa? Zoe? Someone else?'

Whoever she is, she looks more bored than concerned by my questions.

'Does it matter?'

I try to read her face to see if she's being serious. Who can tell?

'Of *course* it matters.'

I get a blank stare directed at me.

'Why?'

'Why? Well, because it would be nice to think that when someone tells you something about themselves that it's, you know … got some basis in reality.'

That just earns a dismissive shrug.

'And what's so great about reality?'

'I don't know … it's real.'

She manages a flat smile.

'*Really*?'

I give her back a flat smile of my own.

'Look, I'd just like to know you better. The *real* you. Is that so strange?'

Her eyes flick to me before retreating.

'A bit,' she says mainly to herself. 'But anyway, I don't see your problem. You *knew* all those other stories weren't true. I didn't try to hide it. Like you do realise that you didn't *really* save me from Karen Kratzman, right? And yes, I did make up stories for those other people, but that doesn't mean that what I told you isn't the truth.'

'No, it doesn't. Except some of it obviously isn't.'

'Like what?'

'Okay, you said you went to Kingston Girls College, but you also said you go to the same school as that Vogel clown. So how does that work exactly? Did *his* parents donate a heap of money to the Kingston building fund too? Did that buy him the "flexibility" to be the only male student at an all girls college?'

Frida rubs her forehead then flaps an impatient hand at me.

'All right. Fine. Seeing how you're so obsessed with my schooling, I'll try to explain it to you as simply as I can. Yes, you're right. I don't go to Kingston Girls. Excellent work, Sherlock. Right now I'm at Bradford High. But only till the end of the year. In Grade Twelve I *will* be attending Kingston Girls College because, believe it or not – and I suppose you probably won't – I was actually awarded a boarding scholarship to go there. So yes,

I admit I was a little premature in saying that I was at Kingston *now*. Sorry about that. But you see, I'm so keen to start, that in my head I'm kind of there already. On the other hand, Bradford High is such a shit hole that I try not to think about being there – *ever*. Does that clear it all up for you?'

Not entirely. It sort of answers some questions but raises others. This one for instance.

'So how come you had to wait till you won a scholarship before you went to Kingston?'

'What?'

'Why didn't your "wealthy" parents send you straight to Kingston? If they have all that money, why did they send you to a "shit hole" first? Why did you need to win a scholarship to get in there?'

Another rub of the forehead.

'Okay, you got me again. Maybe my parents aren't *quite* as successful and well-off as I made out. Maybe I just said that to explain how I could be at Kingston and not really look the part. I wish my parents were loaded – that way I wouldn't have to put up with morons like Vogel for another semester.'

'So that's true? He really does go to Bradford with you?'

'Unfortunately, yes. They cater almost exclusively for morons there.'

She stops and holds up her hands like she's showing that she's unarmed.

'There. Now you know the truth and nothing but the truth about my shitty school life. Happy?'

Sort of. But I can see that she isn't, and now I feel bad about interrogating her. Time perhaps to lighten the mood a little.

'Yeah, except I'm still a bit upset about finding out that I didn't really rescue you in kindergarten. I quite liked the idea of being a sandpit hero.'

Frida's face softens a little with the hint of a smile.

'Sorry about that, Robin. But just be grateful you didn't really have to face off with Crazy Karen Kratzman. That wouldn't have been a pleasant experience for you.'

'Wait. Are you saying she was real?'

Frida seems a little caught off guard by the question. There's a hesitation before she answers.

'Yes. Unfortunately. Too real.'

'And her sand-sandwich trick?'

'Yep. That too. *And* the poor little boy who was forced to eat it.'

'And you rescued him?'

'That would be a no,' Frida says with a touch of real regret in her voice. 'I wish I had. But someone else did. Thank goodness.'

'Wow. I can't believe it. Karen Kratzman, the psycho in the sandpit, is real.'

Frida looks out across the Great Court and runs a finger slowly back and forth through the little hanging moons on her right ear.

'She was real, all right. Don't know about the psycho part though,' she says. 'People do what they do ... and are what they are ... for a reason. I'm sure Karen Kratzman had hers. Maybe all that stuff she did was just some kind of a ... coping mechanism. Just her way of dealing with her shitty, screwed-up life.'

'Coping mechanism, hey? Not bad. You should *definitely* reconsider that therapy career. You sound like a natural.'

That wins me a bit of a smile.

'I know plenty of psychology jargon,' she says. 'I have my father to thank for that.'

'But what makes you so sure that Karen Kratzman had a shitty, screwed-up life anyway? Wasn't she only at kindy with you a little while before she was banned?'

That loses me the smile as Frida drifts away into some private world of her own. I wait for her return.

'I bumped into her again,' she says. 'Last year. At a party.'

'You're kidding. Did she bring a plate of sand-sandwiches and try to force-feed them to everyone?'

Frida responds without humour, as if my comment was meant to be taken seriously.

'No. Doubt she could have done that, even if she wanted to. She was in a bad way. Really bad. Totally wasted. I only recognised her when someone mentioned her name. She'd fallen over in the backyard and cut her knee. I tried to help her. We got talking. She did most of it. Told me all about her life. Spilled her guts completely.' Frida grimaces at the memory. 'Literally at the end. Neither one was very pleasant.'

'Why? What did she say?'

Frida looks first at me then at the ground between us. She seems wary and conflicted about sharing Karen Kratzman's story with me. I'm about to let her know that she doesn't have to when her raspy-edged voice starts up, flat and mechanical like she's reciting a shopping list.

'Never knew her father. Brought up by a drug-addict mum who chose her daughter's first day of Grade One to take a fatal overdose. Punted from one shitty orphanage and one shitty foster home to another. Treated more like a slave or a curse than part of a family. Forced to barricade her bedroom door at night to keep out unwanted visitors. Used as an ashtray by one of her foster pervert dads …'

'What?'

Frida stops and looks up at me.

'Payback for refusing to let him take his "artistic" photos of her,' she explains.

'You're joking. And you think she was telling you the truth?'

Frida nods.

'How can you be sure?'

'There were scars.'

She runs her fingers along the inside of her forearm.

'Down here.'

I find myself imagining the hot tip of a cigarette scorching into Frida's delicate, pale skin. The thought jars my nerves and makes me shudder.

'Jesus. What a sick bastard. You're right. He's the psycho, not her. She say anything else?'

Frida looks off into the middle distance as if she's peering back to that night.

'There was some other stuff she was telling me but then all these gatecrashers showed up off their faces and the party started to spin out of control. I decided to leave. There was a group of boys hanging around who I really didn't trust. I warned her about them. Begged her to come with me. Said it was dangerous to stay there. Told her that she could get hurt.'

Frida stays locked in that memory for a second or two before she breaks free.

'You know what Karen Kratzman said after she heard all that?'

I shake my head.

'She said, "Who cares?".'

The smile that crawls onto Frida's face is built of sadness and regret.

'So what happened to her? Do you know?'

'Nothing good,' Frida says. 'That would be my guess, anyway.'

She remains distant and thoughtful for a few more seconds before making a noticeable effort to wrench herself fully out of the past and back into the present.

'So there you go. There you have it. The Karen Kratzman Story. Unless you think I made that up too.'

'No,' I tell her. 'I don't.'

And it's true. I believe her. I wasn't thinking that at all. But what I *was* thinking was that this whole conversation was actually supposed to be about me getting to know the real Frida better. Where did that idea go? How did the last ten minutes end up being about someone else? How did Frida somehow get replaced by Karen Kratzman? Did she do it on purpose? Have I been deliberately outmanoeuvred and sidetracked here? There's really no way of knowing, so I try not to let those thoughts get to me. But of course they do.

'Well, thanks for sharing all that. At least now I can say I know the real Karen Kratzman a bit better.'

Frida's face sets hard and she takes a step my way. A finger is aimed at my face.

'You know, besides your name, your best friend's name, where you go to school and the fact that you have lofty dreams of becoming a town planner – all of which *I'm* willing to accept and believe by the way – I don't know that much about *you* either. So instead of this whole pot and kettle thing that you have going on, why don't you just show me how it's done, hey?'

'What do you mean?'

'Well, why don't you go first and tell me all about *you* and *your* amazing family?'

'Okay. Sure. No problem. What do you want to know?'

I'm trying my best to look and sound totally relaxed and unconcerned about what she's just suggested.

Which would be easy, if it was true.

20. THE SIBLING

It's Frida's idea to find a better place to talk, so we leave the Great Court and take a path that leads from the main university ring road through bushy parkland to the big campus lake. Off to the side of the path, under a fig tree, we find a bench.

Frida presents it to me by sweeping her hands over it like a game show hostess.

'Ah, all the better for talking,' she says.

And suddenly I feel like I'm being invited to make myself comfortable on a psychiatrist's couch.

From the bench we have a wide view of the lake. It's ringed with reeds and water lilies and dotted with ducks and other waterbirds. Over near the far bank a series of fountains spray misty columns of white water high into the air. In the middle of the lake is an island draped over by a clump of large weeping willows. A flock of white birds is gathering in and around the branches. In the sharp afternoon light they glow like they're lit from inside. Frida and I take our time to soak up the scene before us. She is the first to comment.

'It's beautiful.'

I look at her. With her bleached hair and white clothes, she's glowing like the birds. I agree with her about the view. We sit that way for a while longer before her questions begin.

'So, your family then. Parents?'

'Yep. Regulation mother and father. One of each. Jim and Ester.'

'And what do they do?'

'Dad's a lumberjack. Mum's a mortician.'

Frida sneers a lip at me.

'Yes, and I've heard their son's a first class smart-arse. Now would you like to answer the question?'

I think that's a bit rich coming from her, but I do what she asks.

'Dad's a surveyor. Mum's an accountant.'

I see her trying to hold back a smile.

'What?' I ask.

'A surveyor and an accountant? They must have been absolutely stunned and mortified when they found out they'd given birth to a town planner.'

'And yes, folks, the sarcastic town planner put-downs keep right on coming.'

Frida just laughs and goes back to looking at the birds and the lake.

'And you get on okay? You and your parents?'

It's not really the sort of question I was expecting.

'Yeah, I guess. Why?'

'Just wondered. You know, because of the way you freaked out back there with the fire extinguisher and the security guy, and what Tolly said about your parents not handling the gay protest thing as well as his. I figured they were either super strict Gestapo types, or religious extremists or weird cult leaders and you were frightened of doing something wrong in case they found out.'

That makes me smile. Even though I guess the last part isn't exactly a million miles off the mark.

'No. I can promise you my parents aren't Nazis or religious nutters. And I don't think I can recall them ever claiming to be living gods or boasting about being able to survive just on air. Sorry to disappoint you. We're a fairly boring, normal family, actually.'

Frida nods as she processes that piece of information.

'Normal, eh? So what's that mean, then? They love you and you love them?'

I've never been asked a question like that before. It feels strange saying the answer out loud.

'Pretty much. Yeah.'

'Good for you,' Frida says quietly before pushing on. 'So, siblings? Any brothers or sisters in your happy, boring, normal family?'

There's a tightening in my chest but I answer as matter-of-factly as I can.

'No sisters. One brother.'

'What's his name?'

'Connor.'

'Younger or older?'

'Older.'

'How much?'

And there it is. Once it would have been such an easy question to answer. Now it involves some sidestepping on my part.

'He was born eight years before I was.'

Faint lines form on Frida's forehead.

'Right. Okay. So, he's eight years older, then.'

I'm not sure why I don't just agree with this statement and let it stand. Why I think I need to clarify things and reply with the two words that I'm about to? Maybe I'm just accepting the inevitable. Or maybe it has something to do with the fuzzy softness of Frida's voice and the way the big white birds are gliding lazily around the willow trees and glowing on the branches.

'He *was*,' I say, and that last word hangs there for a fraction of a second before exploding like a flare.

I can sense Frida's eyes peeling away layers from me, even if I can't see them. Just as she did with Tolly's nickname, she quickly uncovers the truth.

'He died,' she says.

It sounds so true and simple that I say it myself.

'He died.'

'I'm sorry.'

She stops asking questions then. It's like a door's clicked open, and for the present at least, she's willing to sit back and wait for whatever might come through.

'That's okay. It was four years ago now. He was killed in a car accident,' I tell her. 'He was twenty. I was twelve. So yeah, he *was* eight years older than me, but now he's only half that.'

I keep my eyes on the birds but I know that they're not the only ones being watched. I wait to see if Frida is going to say something. She doesn't, and more and more I feel the need to fill the silence with words of my own.

'You know what the weird thing about it is? When I was little I used to wish I could catch up with Connor so we'd be the same age. I think at one point I might have actually thought that was possible.'

It makes me smile to imagine that strange, lost version of myself.

'But now, in a few more years, I guess I'll get my wish. After that, I suppose I'll be the older brother.'

There's a gap before the husky warmth of Frida's voice floats in from beside me.

'It must have been hard. Losing someone so close to you like that.'

The air is still and the yellowing tinge of the afternoon light is giving everything an unnatural stage-lighting feel. I know there are other people and other sounds behind us. But right now, here on this bench, all I'm really aware of are our two voices and the random calling of the birds.

'It was. But … we weren't that close. Not at the end,' I tell her. 'Hadn't been for a long time, really.'

She doesn't push me for an explanation but I know I'm going to give one anyway. I can't help myself. Maybe there are some things that I need to finally hear myself say out loud.

'He had his problems, Connor. Big problems. He always seemed to be in trouble for something.'

I sit forward and rest my elbows on my legs.

'After he quit school in Grade Ten, it just got worse and worse. Drinking, fighting, smashing things up, getting sacked from job after job, getting arrested for trying to steal stuff to buy drugs, assault. Mum and Dad were terrified he'd end up killing himself or someone else. There was this fear in their eyes all the time. Connor put that there. After a while I hated him for it.'

I feel my voice waver as the old emotions start to take hold, so I stop talking. Frida lets the silence wash over us for a time before she speaks.

'Sounds like your brother needed help. Professional help.'

She's right, of course.

'Yeah, he did. Definitely. And Mum and Dad tried everything. Sometimes it looked like it was working, too, and he'd promise he'd stick with whatever program he was on or whatever medication he was taking. My parents believed him every time. And every time he let them down. Every single time. I hated him for that as well.'

The memories of those failures are old scars still not properly healed, and I have to stop myself from tearing and raking at them.

'In the end, I just got to the point where I wanted him out of our lives. Wanted him to go away somewhere and leave us alone. Got that wish too.'

'The car accident?' Frida says, holding another door open for me. I walk through and the images from that night unfold one after the other in my head.

'Yeah. It was Connor's birthday. We hadn't heard from him for a few weeks. My parents and I were at home waiting to see if he'd turn up. We had some presents and Mum had made a special birthday dinner like she always did, just in case. The police turned up instead. Told us Connor had sped straight through a random breath testing unit. He'd sideswiped a police car and almost hit some of the cops. So they chased after him. A couple of hundred metres further on there was a sharp bend and Connor tried to take it way too fast. His car left the road and smashed through the front of a brick house. Didn't have a seatbelt on. Killed him instantly. That's what the police said, anyway.'

'God. How awful,' Frida whispers.

I have to brace myself to tell the next bit.

'The room the car hit was a kid's bedroom. A little two-year-old girl was asleep in there.'

I hear a quick intake of breath from beside me.

'They found her buried under all this plaster and bricks and crap. She was alive, but she had cuts and bruises all over her body and concussion and a broken arm. It was just dumb luck she survived. If he'd killed that little girl …'

I stop because the anger is choking my words and strangling my voice. I sit up and let my lungs fill. Another drawn-out silence follows as I stare out into the growing pink of the afternoon sky.

'I know my parents will never get over losing him. You wouldn't expect them to. But I thought at least the fear might disappear from their eyes. It hasn't though. Not completely. They try to hide it, but I can still see it sometimes … especially when they look at me.'

Frida twists my way. There's a question scrawled across her face.

'Your parents are worried that you might turn into your brother?'

The aggression in my voice leaps out before I can stop it.

'I'm *not* my brother,' I growl at her.

No, maybe not. But right now, I sound a hell of a lot like him.

21. The Memories

'Hey, whatever happened to that coffee you promised me?'

'Sure. Sorry. Coming right up.'

It's been a while since either of us has said anything, and I'm happy for the chance to move on. I think we both are. We leave the bench and set off for the main cafeteria, but on the way there we pass a mobile coffee van selling homemade cakes and muffins. A few small tables and chairs are scattered about a terraced area. I point to the handwritten sign promoting a half-price coffee and food combo for school students with photo ID.

'Sounds pretty good. What do you think?'

'Ah, yeah, fine,' Frida says, looking around. 'Less crowded and noisy here anyway.'

'Great. Got your student card on you?'

'Yeah ... but you go ahead and order what you want first ... and I'll grab us a table. I can get mine after you.'

It doesn't really seem necessary to me because the place isn't that busy, but Frida's already zeroing in on a table on the edge of the terrace. It's not long before we're sitting opposite each other, sipping hot coffee and dividing up a bulging blueberry muffin and a large slab of banana bread.

In my head I'm still going over everything I've said about Connor. Apparently Frida is too. She breaks off a chunk of muffin and lifts it towards her mouth. Then she stops as if she's had a light bulb moment.

'That song you played for me. It's about your brother.'

It's more of a statement than a question, but I let her know that she's right.

'*How am I meant to turn the page?* It's about what happened to him and trying to move on, isn't it? Trying to get your life back together.'

I confirm that as well.

'Not a bad image.'

I get in early to beat her to the punch.

'For a town planner?' I suggest.

She laughs. 'You said it, not me.'

'Well, thanks anyway. But I suppose I should come clean. I sort of borrowed-slash-stole that line from my grandmother.'

'From your grandmother?'

'Yep. Nanna Rose.'

Frida holds up a hand.

'Wait. Stop right there. Nanna Rose? Your grandmother's called Nanna Rose. What's your grandfather called, then? Please, I need to know.'

'Poppy Bob.'

'It just gets better and better.'

She's smirking and making fun of me. But I don't mind. I like to see her smile. I like the way her thin top lip curves. And the dimples that make brief appearances. I keep finding new things to like about her.

'You think *that's* funny?' I tell her. 'My other grandparents are called Beavis and Butthead.'

I say it just as she's had a sip of coffee, and she has to clamp one hand over her mouth and flap the other one about like a broken propeller just to stop herself spraying it everywhere. Gold. Better than gold.

When she finally recovers, her face is red and she tries to look annoyed, but it's obvious she's still battling to keep it together. Eventually she regains enough composure to narrow her eyes at me.

'So, before we got sidetracked, you were about to tell me the story of how you shamefully ripped off your poor old granny's intellectual property.'

'Was I?'

'Yes, you were, because you know how much I love stories.'

Yes, I certainly do. Except maybe true ones that are about you, I'm thinking. But I keep that thought to myself.

'Well, okay. Confession time, then. I was at Nanna Rose's place mowing her lawn one day and maybe she knew I wasn't coping too well with the whole Connor thing, because after I finished and we were having something to eat, she brings out this old photo album of hers and shows me a shot of her first husband. The guy she was married to before she married my mum's dad.'

'That would be Poppy Bob.' Another smirk. I ignore it.

'Right. Well done. Anyway, you think Vogel's a prick? Well, Nanna Rose's first husband was a total bastard. Sent her to hospital a few times.'

Frida's face sets hard.

'Luckily they were only together for a few years, and then he was killed when a tractor tipped over on him. Nan says it explains her love of farm machinery.'

Frida nods approvingly.

'I think I'd like your Nanna Rose. But why keep a photo of that guy?'

'That's exactly what I asked her, and she said she kept it there because it was no use pretending he never existed and besides, she liked to be able to look that mongrel in the eyes and then start turning the pages – the ones filled with much better and happier memories – and bury the bastard in the past. She reckoned I needed to do the same thing. She said Connor's death was sad, but nothing was going to change that or make it go away, so I had to face up to it, accept it, and start turning the pages.'

Frida is staring into her coffee cup.

'Nice thought,' she says. 'But not as simple as it sounds, I'd imagine.'

I think back to the time right after Conner's death and how I felt.

'No. It's not. When Connor died, it was like … everything just stopped and nothing meant anything or made sense any more. It felt like we were going to be frozen and trapped like that forever. I didn't think any of us would ever move on.'

A thought occurs to me then that's so weird it makes me smile.

'A bit like being that black blob in Tolly's amazing Pitch Drop Experiment.'

Frida peers down into her cup and tilts it back and forth. 'And someone just has to tap you and you shatter,' she says to the dregs of her coffee.

When she lifts her head, our eyes meet and hold together.

'Getting a bit morbid here, aren't we?' she says. 'Maybe it's time *we* moved on and turned over the page to something a little more positive. Like, I've heard the bad stuff, how about you tell me something really good about your brother? I know, what's your favourite ever happy memory of him? You must have one.'

An image of Connor in our family lounge room fills my mind. His face is calm and he's concentrating. He's even allowing himself to smile.

'Too easy,' I tell her. 'There was this one time when we hadn't heard from him for months and then one night he just shows up out of the blue at our house looking heaps better than he'd been for ages. We found out that he'd been interstate at some drug rehabilitation place. Anyway, it was just a couple of days after my birthday and I was in the lounge room playing the new guitar Mum and Dad had got me. Connor had forgotten all about my birthday, of course, but when he saw me, he went upstairs and dug out his old guitar and started tuning it with mine. Have you ever done that? Tuned two guitars together?'

'Well, you've seen my guitar-playing skills. What do you think?'

'I'll take that as a firm no. Okay. So here's the thing. If you play two strings together and they're out of tune, you can hear it because you get this wavy vibration sound like the different notes are fighting against each other. But as you keep adjusting one of the strings and they come closer, the wavy vibrations slow down more and more until eventually they disappear altogether, and the two strings become one sound. That's when those two strings are in tune. You just do that for all the strings and you're done.'

Frida smiles. 'Thanks for the lesson. How much do I owe you?'

'The first one's always on the house,' I tell her. 'But you asked for my favourite memory of Connor, and that's how it started that night. Just the two of us, sitting there, tuning our guitars. We hadn't done anything together for years, and it just felt like all the shit and craziness that had built up between us was being smoothed away and Connor and I were being pulled closer too. Like it wasn't just the guitars that were getting back in tune. I guess that sounds really stupid.'

'No,' Frida says. 'More beautiful than stupid, I would have thought.'

I look at Frida's thoughtful, serious face. The disappearing sun is giving her pale skin a warm glow. If this was one of those romcom films that I was fantasising about this morning, and if I was any sort of a leading man, this would be the scene and the moment where I'd tell her what *I* find beautiful. But obviously it's not, and certainly I'm not, so I finish my story instead.

'Anyway, after we tuned the guitars, we played some songs together. We sounded pretty good too. Connor even joked about us going on the road. And when Mum and Dad came in to listen, there was no fear in their eyes. Just happiness. We must have played for a couple of hours until Connor started to get a bit jumpy and he left. But yeah, that night, tuning the guitars, talking a bit, singing and playing those songs, just him and me, that's definitely my favourite Connor memory by far. I never wanted that night to end.'

Frida touches her hand on my arm then moves it away.

'That's a lovely memory. It really is. I hope you got the chance to do it again.'

'Just once,' I say. 'A few weeks before he died.'

And before I can stop it, that memory comes crashing back in.

Our lounge room. Me. Home alone. Playing guitar. Connor stumbling in. Wild. Agitated. Pulling out drawers. Searching for money. Throwing stuff about. Leaving the room. Back now, his old guitar in one hand. Knocking it against walls and furniture. Tripping his way to me. Sitting close. Too close. His eyes crazed and frantic. Struggling to tune his guitar to mine. Turning the wrong key. Turning the right key the wrong way. Or too much. Way too much. Shouting at me that he knows what he's doing. Spit hanging on his chin. Wrenching at the keys now. Twisting them. Punching them. Cutting his knuckles. Bleeding. Grabbing and thrashing at the strings. Wilder. Angrier. More agitated. Lurching to his feet. Guitar raised above his head. Bringing it down. Smashing it on the table top. Again. Again. Just strings and dangling, jagged pieces left. Panting. Sweating. Eyes blazing. Blazing at me. Blazing at my arms wrapped around my guitar. My new guitar. My first guitar. My birthday present. Me shouting. Begging. No. No, please. Please don't. The guitar ripped away. Torn away. My new guitar. My first guitar. My birthday present. Swung high. Swung hard. Smashed. Smashed. And smashed again. Pieces flung at

149

my face. Kicking aside furniture. A parting curse. A slamming door. Silence. Silence. Silence. Our lounge room. Just me again. Alone. But crying now.

'Was that a good memory too?' Frida asks me.

I see a hint of fear in her eyes as she awaits my answer. But there's something else there as well. Hope.

'Maybe not *quite* as good,' is all I say.

22. THE STUDENT CARD

I think I've finally worked out what Frida's super power is. Getting other people to talk. Her father would be proud. The psychiatrist more so than the lumberjack or senator. But there's definitely been too much one-way traffic. Time I think for someone else to do some sharing.

'So what about you and your family, then? Any brothers or sisters?'

She wraps her hands around her coffee cup.

'No.'

'No one?'

'Nope. Just little ole me. And my parents, of course. But I've already told you about them.'

Yes, you certainly have. You've told me that they're wealthy, then maybe not so wealthy. They're either happily married, or according to your Acoustic Society story, divorced *and* that your mother is a painter or possibly an actor and then of course there's your father, the psychiatric senator and part-time lumberjack.

I wait to give her the chance to add something. Anything. I even use her raised-eyebrows technique against her to make it clear that I'm keen and open to hearing more. But there is no more. She moves her lips quickly in and out of a smile, breaks off a piece of banana bread and chews it in slow motion.

'This is *so* good,' she moans. 'Banana bread is the Rolls Royce of bread. IMHO.'

It's too much. I can't hold back the sarcasm dump that has built up inside me.

'Great to know. Thanks *so* much for being *trusting* enough to share your intimate thoughts about banana bread with me. I *really* feel like I know you now.'

Frida lowers what's left of the banana bread to her plate. She thrusts her jaw my way and fights sarcasm with sarcasm.

'Well, I'm sorry for being an only child. I apologise. I realise how *selfish* it is of me not having any stories to share with you about my *non-existent* siblings. I suppose I could always make up some imaginary ones for you if you like, but I sort of picked up the vibe that you were anti that sort of thing and were more into reality. Or would you like me to call my parents and ask them to get busy with it and whip up a couple of siblings just for you? Would that make you happy? Might take a while though. Are you prepared to wait?'

And I return fire.

'Would that be your rich parents or your not-so-rich ones? And by the way, I never did find out. Are they still a painter and psychiatrist or has that changed again too? FBI agent and astronaut now, perhaps? Drag queen and drug lord?'

I know as soon as I say it that I've gone too far. Frida's face is closing down and some kind of invisible wall is going up between us. She fires some final words at me before she retreats behind it.

'Hey, just because you told me about your brother, doesn't mean I owe you anything. I didn't force you to do that. That was all *your* choice.'

We sit in silence, avoiding eye contact. I finish my coffee then pick at the last of the muffin. It's hard to swallow now. I rack my brain trying to think of something to say to open up the communication channels again. What I come up with is pretty lame.

'I'd better text Tolly and let him know where we are. That Q and A thing must be about finished.'

Frida doesn't react in any way so I drag out my phone and take my time sending the message. At least it gives me something to do. A reply comes straight back.

'Tolly says it's still going strong. Says he'll either meet us right outside A6 or if we're not there, he'll come here.'

Once again I get zero feedback from Frida. It's like her good ear has now shut up shop as well. At least to me. I push back in my chair and squeeze my phone into the front pocket of my jeans. As I do, something on the ground under the table catches my eye. It's a face-down ID card. I quickly check that I still have mine. I do.

'Hey, did you drop your student card?' I ask Frida at the same time as I'm reaching under the table.

A flash of emotion pulses across her otherwise stony face. I'm not sure what it is. She looks under the table to where my hand is heading.

'Yes, that's mine. Leave it. It's fine. I'll get it. I'll get it.'

Too late. It's already in my hand.

'No problem. I got it.'

'Thanks. Just give it here. Give it to me. Don't look at it. Please.'

153

There's a growing urgency in her voice. Panic almost. I bring the card up to the table. My fingers are closed around it.

What's she so worried about? Why doesn't she want me to look at her student card? What doesn't she want me to see? Or know? Don't tell me that the whole going to Bradford thing is just another one of her made-up stories.

'What's wrong?' I ask her.

'Nothing. Nothing's wrong. I just want you to give me my student card, that's all. Is that such a big deal? Is that too much to ask?'

She's angry now. But also afraid. Why? It's just an ID card. What is there to be frightened of? She draws in a breath to calm herself down. The strain on her face eases marginally.

'Look, it's just the picture of me, okay? I know it's stupid, but I hate it. That's all. At the start of the year, right before our class photos, my skin decided to have this mega pimple breakout. It was disgusting. Like I had the pox or something. Worst photo ever. Vogel and his mates tease me about it all the time. So *please* don't look at it. It's revolting and so embarrassing. Just hand it over. Please.'

I study her face. Her pale, clear skin is dusted with a few light freckles and marked only by the faint scar on the bridge of her nose. She's stopped talking but her eyes are still pleading with me. I move my hand forward to pass the card over.

I'm not sure why I do the next thing.

Maybe it's because I'm just fed up with all the mystery surrounding her and all the stories she's been hiding behind. Maybe it's because I just need to know if she's telling me the truth, and for the first time I'm holding some proof right here in my hand. Maybe after all I've told her about Connor, I think I've earned the right.

None of that makes it right, of course. But it's not enough to stop me.

I flip the card over and look down at it.

The Bradford High crest and the Bradford name are the first things I see. So that much is true.

Frida's photo is the next thing I take in. It's not the best image in the world, I'll give her that. It's more police mug shot than glamour magazine. But her fair skin is perfectly clear.

'I don't know what you're talking about,' I tell her. 'There's nothing wrong with your photo. You look fine. A bit on the grim and grumpy side maybe, a bit like you've been detained against your will, but if you think *that's* bad, you should ...'

And that's when I see it. It's so obvious I wonder why it's taken me this long.

I look from the image on the ID card to the live version in front of me where a churning mix of shock and fear is quickly fusing into anger.

The ID is snatched from my hand.

The one belonging to Karen Kratzman.

23. THE PHONE CALL

A torn, icy voice hits me like a slap in the face.

'That'd be right. Don't listen to me. Go ahead. Just do whatever *you* want.'

She pushes her chair back with a screech and stands up. She's gathering up her things.

'Wait. Where're you going?'

'Away from you.'

'No, don't. Stay, please. I'm sorry. I shouldn't have looked. Can't we just … start again?'

She doesn't answer me. Instead she throws her water bottle into her bag and loops it over her shoulder. I go to grab my stuff as well. The icy voice returns. Stronger. More fierce.

'Don't you *dare* follow me. Do you hear what I'm saying? I want you to leave me alone. Can you do that? Can you do what *I* want this time? Huh? Are you *capable* of that?'

The strength in her voice falters at the end. She blinks away the emotion in her eyes and clenches her jaw. I lower myself back into my seat and stay there as she weaves a path between the other tables, then continues down the ring road and vanishes into a laneway between two buildings.

Every part of me wants to leap up and chase after her. But I don't. I can't. So I keep my eyes glued on that laneway entrance hoping that one of the people exiting from it might be her changing her mind.

They're not.

I remain seated, debating with myself over what to do now. Should I just wait here or should I go after her? I decide I have to stay put. It's what she's asked me to do. Maybe if I give her time to herself, she'll calm down a bit and if I'm still here, then at least she'll know where to find me. It's a plan, a pretty depressing and crap one, but it's all I have.

The Open Day has begun to wind down and there are nowhere near as many people about. The late afternoon light has lost its sharp edge now, and everything is taking on that stale, washed-out, dying-day kind of look. Pretty appropriate given the circumstances and how I'm feeling. I stare at the vacant chair opposite me. The world suddenly feels a lot emptier than just that one small space. I push my chair back and bend forward until my head is resting on the table top. The metal surface is cool against my forehead. I close my eyes. It helps me focus on just how much of an idiot I am and how monumentally I've stuffed things up. What's that expression again? Ah, yes. Sad, pathetic prick. Still fits me like a glove.

I can't get the image of that ID card and the name on it out of my mind. All day I've been trying to put together a jigsaw puzzle called Frida, but now it's been completely blown apart and there are all these new pieces now, pieces that I thought belonged to someone else's picture. How do they all go together? Where do things like a faint scar, a broken voice, a damaged ear and 'friends' who never seem to appear, fit in? And is that a picture I really want to see?

I'm still struggling with these questions when a scrape of chair legs on concrete and a jolt and wobble of the table bring me back to the here and now. I'm no longer alone. Is it possible that my crap and depressing plan of waiting and hoping she'll come back has actually worked? I jerk my head up.

Nope. Not even close.

Tolly thrusts out his bottom lip and pats me on the head.

'Awwww. Past your bedtime already, little fella?'

'Yeah, that's really hilarious.'

'You're too kind,' he says, looking around. 'So. No Frida?'

I sit back and throw up my hands.

'No. And you know why? Because I'm a dick of immense proportions.'

Tolly levels an accusing finger at me.

'Look, this is no time to start big-noting yourself,' he says, then places a hand on my shoulder. 'You seem to be a little upset. Why don't you tell Uncle Tolly all about it? Come on. Spill.'

I'm not much in the mood for joking around or being patronised. Or even talking, for that matter. But I know from past experience that Tolly won't back off, so I decide to just get it over with and tell him everything that's happened while he's been away. It's not fun. Having to revisit the whole Karen Kratzman story and explain how I came to see that name on a student card leave me feeling even more crap than I already was.

'I stuffed up big time, Tolly.'

'Love to disagree with you, buddy, but … you know … weight of evidence and all. So what are you going to do?'

'Stay here and see if she comes back. What else can I do?'

'And if she doesn't? Then what? You haven't got much time.

My father's picking us up in a half an hour or so.'

I'd already come to a decision about that when my head was on the table.

'I'm not leaving, Tolly. I can't. I'll hang around here for a while longer and if she doesn't turn up I'll start wandering around and see if I can find her. Maybe she'll see me and want to talk. Although I seriously doubt it. But I have to do something. When she left she was really angry and upset … and hurt. Because of me. *I* did that to her.'

I look at Tolly. He's nodding his head like he's listening to some slow and steady inner beat.

'And it will not stand?'

'No. It will not,' I tell him. 'So, do you want to stay too? Help me find her?'

'Love to, my friend. But can't. Big family reunion do at our place tonight. I am forbidden to miss it under pain of death and as the good son that I am, I cannot go against my parents' threats. Plus, they're paying me a shitload of money to serve drinks, so it would be unfair and irresponsible of me to let them down.'

'Okay, sure, no problem. Just tell your dad that I've decided to stay.'

Tolly throws back his head and mimes hysterical laughter at the sky. He stops as suddenly as he begins.

'Yeah, well, that's definitely not gonna happen, is it?'

'Why not?'

'Because, young Sebastian, *you* know your parents and *I* know your parents and my *father* knows your parents. Even more to the point, all of us know your *mother*. And we all understand that the only reason she doesn't literally pack you in cotton wool every time you step out of the house is because she would probably get reported to Children's Services. So there's no way known that my father is going to leave here without you unless he hears it straight from one of your parents' mouths. Therefore, the only way this is going to play out is for you to ring them now, inform them that you're staying on, get their official okey-dokey and then have them ring my father to officially okey-dokey it all with him.'

'Look, can't you just …'

Tolly pushes a finger over my lips.

'Hush! Ring. Now. And remember that I'm listening to your every word. Do exactly as I've said and nobody gets hurt.'

He's absolutely right about my mother, of course, which only makes me feel more pissed off with him. I swipe his hand away, yank out my phone and wave it in front of his face.

'Happy?'

'Ring your father. It'll be easier.'

'Wow. Really? Like I hadn't figured *that* out already.'

I hit my father's name in the Contacts list and listen to the ring tone. It goes on quite a while before a voice answers. I close my eyes.

'Oh, yeah, hi … *Mum.*'

I open them but only so I can glare at Tolly.

'No, Mum. Nothing's wrong … No, don't bother getting him out of the shower. It's not that important. I just wanted to let you both know something … No, I'm not in trouble … Nothing's happened … Yeah, I'm still at uni … Yes, everything's fine … Yes, I'm with Warren.'

Tolly leans forward.

'Hi, Mrs Benet!'

'That was him all right ... Yes, I'll tell him.'

I power up another glare at Tolly.

'*Hi right back at you, Warren.* But Mum, look, I just rang to let you know ...'

Time to fill the lungs and take the plunge.

'... I'm not coming home with Warren and Mr Pearce. I'm staying on here at uni for a bit longer, so you need to ring Warren's parents and let *them* know that *you* know, okay? ... No, I told you already *nothing's* wrong. Why does anything have to be wrong? ... No, he's not staying ... Well, because he's got some family reunion thing to go to at his place ... I just told you why. Because I just want to hang around a bit longer, that's all. There's stuff I haven't seen yet ... Yeah, I know I've been here all day, but it's a big place and there's lots of information to take in. You want me to make a good choice for my future, don't you? ... Yes, all the talks and presentations are over. But there's other stuff as well. Like there's a concert on pretty soon ... Yeah well, I might not be alone, because I sort of met this girl ...'

Tolly does an imitation of that kid from *Home Alone*, clutching his face and screaming silently.

'Just someone I met, that's all. She goes to ... Kingston Girls College.'

Tolly arches an eyebrow and looks down his long nose at me. He holds out a hand and wobbles it about to signify the dubious nature of my last statement.

'She's nice, Mum. You'd like her.'

Tolly leans forward again.

'I can vouch for that, Mrs B. In fact she's way too good for your son. *Waaaaaaaay* too good.'

I shove him back.

'How would I know what he's talking about? It's just Warren being his usual pain-in-the arse self ... Well, it hardly qualifies as swearing, but anyway is that all okay, then? I'll catch a bus from here to the city and another one from there, home ... Yeah, there's plenty. Every fifteen minutes or so. Remember how you checked last night in case something happened and we couldn't get picked up ... No, I'll be fine. Look, I probably won't end up staying that long anyway ... Yeah, yeah, okay, no problem. I'll text you when I'm on the first bus ... Okay *and* the second one ... No, Mum. It's a five-minute walk from our bus stop. I think you can survive till I get home before you hear from me again ... Okay, great, now don't forget. You need to ring Warren's parents straightaway before they head off and let them know they're not picking me up ... Yes, for the millionth time, I'll be fine. Don't worry ... Yes, I know, it's your job to worry. Just don't worry *obsessively*. Or at least not *excessively* obsessively ... Right, Mum. Listen to me. Mum. Listen. I'm going to hang up now. I'll see you later on ... Yes, I know I can always ring you to pick me up if I need to, but I won't need to because like I've told you now a million and one times already, I'll be absolutely fine ... Yeah. Okay. Love you too.'

Tolly's face looms close again.

'Love you *three*, Mrs Benet!'

'Yes, Mum. We all do. He's just so ... *lovable*. Okay, bye. And

162

Mum. It's stupid and unnecessary and you really need to back off a bit and stop doing it … but thanks for worrying.'

Opposite me, Tolly is grabbing at his heart and wiping a flood of pretend tears from his eyes.

'Oh, and Mum. One more thing. When you ring Mr Pearce tell him that I saw *Casablanca* on the big screen here today.'

Tolly stops the pretend waterworks and commences an elaborate mime of loading a rifle and pointing it at me.

'Yeah, it *is* good. Be sure to tell Mr Pearce that he *must* make Warren watch it.'

Tolly jerks back as he fires off a couple of rounds. I pretend to brush them aside.

'Okay, see ya later.'

I hang up and Tolly slaps his hands on the table.

'Well, how easy was that? Right. Well, I've still got a bit of time to kill, so first I'm going to get a drink and a couple of those awesome half-priced muffins over there and then when I come back, I'll give you the message.'

By the time his words sink in and register with me, he's already halfway to the counter of the mobile coffee van.

'Hey, what message?' I call after him.

He stops. He's got the why-are-you-asking-me-such-a-dumb-question look on his face that I'm so familiar with.

'The message that the-girl-formerly-known-as-Frida asked me to pass on to you, of course.'

24. THE MESSAGE

Tolly is still in the motion of sitting back down when I begin bombarding him with all the questions that have been bouncing around in my head for the last few minutes.

'You talked to her? Where? How? Why didn't you tell me? Was she all right? What was the message?'

He peels the wrapper back on one of his muffins, takes a big bite and hums with pleasure. When he speaks it's with a ridiculous French accent and equally ridiculous hand gestures.

'Mmmmm. It's coooooooked to parfeeeeeeection. It's just meeeelt in maaaar moooouth!'

'Tolly!'

'Okay, okay, okay. She was there waiting for me when I left that Q and A thing.'

'Waiting for you? Are you sure? Actually *waiting* for you? She didn't just maybe bump into you accidentally?'

'No. I'm certain she was waiting for me.'

'Why?'

'Well, two reasons. One – she was sitting on the bench right outside the lecture theatre. And two – just something she said.'

'What?'

'She said, "I've been waiting for you".'

I try to remain composed. It's not easy.

'Great. Right. Fine. You got me. Good one. So, what was she like? Did she seem okay? What did she say? What was the message?'

'She was a bit … on the serious side. She told me that you two had a fight about something but wouldn't say what. Then she said she had a message for me to give to you and that I had to remember it word for word.'

'And did you?'

By the look on Tolly's face it's clear that he's just been grossly insulted.

'Who was it who memorised the entire Periodic Table as well as all the world capitals *and* all the US states and every US president and every Australian prime minister while he was still in primary school? Who was it who successfully completed the online Extreme Brain Training program? And which of the two people sitting at this table right now would you say possesses an almost photographic memory?'

'That would be you, you and, let me think, you. Now just tell me what the message was!'

'No problem. She said …' Tolly's eyes wander away. He frowns and sucks on his teeth. 'Nuh, sorry. It's gone.'

I thump the table. People look. I lean forward and lower my voice.

'Tolly, why are you being such a jerk-off? This is important to me. Tell me exactly what she said. Now.'

'Okay, she said, and I'm quoting *verbatim* here, "Tell Sebastian that if you really want to start again you must go back to the start".'

'Finally! Thank you. Why didn't you just say that as soon as you got here?'

'Once again, two reasons. One, I was asked by the message

giver to allow her a bit of time to get to where she wanted to go to *before* I passed on her message, and two, you needed to do some penance for being, as you quite rightly pointed out, a dick of immense proportions.'

Hard to argue with that.

'Lovely. And that's it? That's everything? When she gave you the message, she just left?'

'Yep. Straight after she kissed me.'

I wait to see if he's joking, but Tolly seems more interested in polishing off the remains of his first muffin and moving on to attack number two.

'She *kissed* you?'

'Uh huh. Right here,' he says, pointing to his left cheek. 'Said I was a superhero. I told her I was majorly shattered about my cover being blown.'

'I think that kiss might have been for what you did to Vogel.'

Tolly stops chewing, thinks for a bit, then holds up a finger.

'*Or* she might have just been overcome, as *so* many have before her, by my irresistible animal magnetism.'

'Yes. Or that. Now back to the message. You sure that's everything she said?'

'The whole kit and most of the caboodle. So, do you know what it means?'

'Well, yeah, I think so. Seems pretty straightforward. If you want to start again, you must go back to the start. Well, the start has to be where we met today, doesn't it? So that's in the foyer of the movie theatre. She must mean for me to meet her at the Hub. What else could it be?'

Tolly pulls a face and hunches up his shoulders.

'*Seems* logical.'

I don't want to waste any more time discussing it, so I jump up and grab my backpack.

'Okay, Tolly. Wish me luck. I'll give you a ring tomorrow. Let you know how it all went.'

'Ah, tell you what,' he says, 'I'm going to be here for a bit longer anyway, so why don't you text me and let me know if she's there or not? I mean, I'm sure she will be there, *but* if she's not, then the message must mean something else, and maybe I can help you work it out. Or, if all else fails, you can still get a lift home with me and Dad.'

To tell you the truth, I'm a bit annoyed and disappointed by my best friend's disturbing lack of faith.

'Yeah. Sure. Whatever. But she'll be there. I know she will.'

Tolly and I bump fists and I set off.

I jog down the ring road and pass the lecture theatre where I lent Helena my pen. Was that even today? It seems like another lifetime ago. I turn at the path that leads to the cafeteria then veer off down some concrete steps to another path that will take me to the Hub theatre. And the foyer. And the girl who's waiting for me there.

How weird is that? A girl in the foyer of a movie theatre waiting for *me* to come through a set of sliding doors. It's like this morning's romcom fantasy, only in reverse. Is it possible that I'm about to get my feel-good, happy ending after all? Or will this just turn out to be another random scene in my mashed-up and crappily edited life?

See, that's the problem I have with Life. It's never just one type of thing, is it? Not like films. With films, you sort of know what you're in for. If it's a sci-fi film, you get space, the future, or aliens. If it's action, you get gun fights and car chases. Horror, you get monsters and ghosts and basically shit-scared. Comedy, you get laughs and happy endings. Romance, you get the girl. Or the guy. Depending on your preference. See what I mean? But it's not the same with life …

With life it's all over the place. One minute it's tears. Next minute it's laughter. Then, just when you think you're headed for a happy ending, the monsters turn up. Or the aliens. Or someone with a gun. And sometimes there's a car chase. With a crash. And someone dies. Yeah, films make a lot more sense to me than life. Plus, they're a lot easier to walk out of or turn off.

And speaking of films.

I round a bend in the path and arrive at the cinema. It's lit up inside now. I bound up the steps of the main entrance two at a time and when the doors slide open I head inside. From where I'm standing I have a good view of the L-shaped foyer and its blue and gold-flecked carpet. The short end of the L is directly in front of me. To my left is the box office and small candy bar, and straight ahead and down a set of steps is the back entrance. The long part of the L is to my right. It's a wide corridor that leads past the entrances to the theatre's two cinemas. At the far end a few tables and chairs are set up in front of a wall plastered with old movie posters.

I stand for a few seconds catching my breath and taking it all in. One thing is immediately obvious. It's this. Besides a guy and a girl flirting with each other inside the box office and another guy wiping down the tables beneath the wall of posters, I'm the only other person here.

Which as romcoms go, doesn't strike me as particularly romantic.

Or comic.

25. THE SEARCH

This can't be right. *I'm* at the start. So where is *she*?

I march straight ahead and down the steps to the back doors of the theatre. Outside there's a circular drive and a small car park. Beyond that a road runs down between playing fields on one side and a big sports pavilion and multiple tennis courts on the other. I walk to the end of the circular drive and take a good look around. No one's there. Unless you count the crows mocking me from the overhead power lines. And I don't.

I go back inside. As I climb the steps I can't help myself. I start wondering if this might be my feel-good, romcom moment coming up right now. You know, I'll walk up the stairs feeling all confused and depressed and when I get to the top the big sliding doors on the main entrance will open up like a stage curtain and there she'll be. Just like in the movies. And she'll look up and smile and I'll smile back and then …

I'm already at the top of the stairs.

The big sliding doors across the foyer look like they're fused shut. I go over to the box office. The guy and the girl behind the counter reluctantly peel apart when they see me coming. Their name tags identify them in a cheerful font as Nick and Jodie.

'Can I help you with anything?' Jodie asks, then shoots a sneaky smile at Nick like it's some kind of sexy in-joke that only they could possibly understand.

'I'm looking for a girl.'

'Aren't we all?' Nick quips. Both Nick and Jodie find this tremendously amusing.

I supply a description. Whitish hair. Long and a bit frizzed out on one side. Darker and shaved close on the other. A bunch of earrings in one ear. White skirt. White top. Pale skin. Dark eyebrows.

They look at each other then shake their heads.

'Sorry,' Jodie says, sounding more bored than heartbroken about it. 'Sounds awesome, but doesn't ring a bell.'

'Could have been here earlier, I suppose,' Nick throws in. 'Our shift's just started. Doug might know.'

He indicates his co-worker wiping down tables at the far end of the foyer. I leave them to get back to their secret groping and head that way.

Doug's an older guy with impossibly brown hair and matching goatee. I feed him the same description as the other two and get pretty much the same response. I look back down the foyer. I can't help it. Every time I turn round I half expect her to be there. How many times is it possible to do this and still keep believing that the *next* time will be different? I know I'm pathetic, but what about the message? *If you want to start again, go back to the start.* Well, here I am. At the start! Ready to start again. So why isn't she here too? It doesn't make any sense.

Unless …

I'm staring at the signs identifying Cinema One and Cinema Two. And isn't this exactly the sort of thing that happens all the time in those feel-good movies? Just when all appears lost, the main character comes up with a brilliant new thought and suddenly everything's back on track. Well, here's my brilliant new thought. She's waiting for me *inside* the cinema! And it makes sense too, because seeing a movie was like the first thing we did together. Just me and her. *And* now that I think about it, it was also inside Cinema One where we finally got around to introducing ourselves properly. It's where I told her that my name was Sebastian. So technically it was inside the cinema, not out here in the foyer, where we first officially met. It's where you could say we started!

'Excuse me. What's showing in Cinema One now?'

I'm asking Doug of the badly dyed hair.

'Cinema One? *Ben-Hur*,' Doug answers without missing a beat in his table wiping.

'How long before the session finishes?'

'About half an hour.'

'Can I just take a quick look inside and see if that girl I asked you about, you know the one I'm looking for, is in there? It won't take long. I'll just be in and out. Please. It's really important.'

Doug isn't too thrilled, but he agrees. I follow him to the entrance to Cinema One.

'Be quick and be quiet,' he says.

It's his final briefing before he opens the door and we both step into the darkness. My eyes adjust quickly. Up on the screen are a bunch of people in togas standing around some chariots. I do a scan of the theatre. It's mostly empty so it doesn't take long to see that she isn't there. I give Doug a thumbs-down signal and we leave. So much for that brilliant thought. Now there's only one other possibility remaining. But I'm not very hopeful.

'What's on in the other cinema?'

'*Star Wars*,' Doug says, already on his way to attack another table.

I chase after him.

'The latest one?'

'First one. The original.'

The very first *Star Wars*? Could that be it? Could that be the 'start' she was talking about all along? The start of the *Star Wars* franchise? Was I supposed to meet her in a galaxy far, far away? Is she testing me to see if I'm smart and creative enough to work it out, or am I reading way too much into it? Doesn't matter either way. I can't leave here not knowing. I have to find out if she's in there or not.

'Can I check Cinema Two out as well?'

Doug reacts like I've asked for a piggyback up Mount Everest.

'I'll be quick. In and out in a flash. Same as last time. Promise.'

Doug does the Mount Everest look one more time so that I'm in no doubt about the scale of the enormous sacrifice he is making. He tosses his cleaning cloth on the table and leads the way to the second cinema. But this time when we get inside, it's a little different.

For a start, the theatre is three-quarters full and a dark, deep-space scene on the screen means it's harder to make out individual people, particularly those furthest away from us. And there's another problem as well. A few people are dressed in *Star Wars* costumes and there's a couple of storm troopers and what I assume is a Chewbacca but could just as easily be a deformed grizzly bear, blocking my view of the people in the seats in front of them. I go further down the stairs. The storm troopers see me and turn my way. Other people wonder what the storm troopers are looking at, and do the same. A hand lands on my back. It belongs to Doug. He's looking concerned.

'I have to go further down,' I whisper to him. 'I can't see everyone properly from here.'

Doug shakes his head at me. Obviously I'm not being quite quiet or quick enough for his liking. He jerks his head in the direction of the exit.

'You've had your look. Come on. Out. Now!'

A heap more people are now watching us. Doug really needs to work on his whispering skills. He takes a firm grip on my shirt and doesn't look like he's going to release it any time soon. Once again he jerks his head towards the exit. I automatically begin to follow him. But with every step questions are blasting out louder and louder inside my skull. What if she's here? Right here. What if she's sitting metres away from me right now and I leave and she never knows that I got her message and came looking for her? What if I spend the rest of my life asking myself those questions and never ever knowing the answers? That's no romcom. That's an over-the-top tear-jerking melodrama!

I can't leave this place with those questions unanswered. I can't. I come to a decision. I wrench my shirt clear of Doug's grasp and bound back down the steps right to the front of the theatre. My eyes are flashing rapidly over the sea of unfamiliar faces. I'm not quite through them when Doug wraps my arm in a death grip and begins dragging me back towards the exit. A space battle is now raging up on the big screen, but for a lot of the audience the contest between Doug and me is now the star attraction.

I'm being pulled away and I haven't been able to check everyone in the theatre. There's only one thing left for me to do now. One thing that will stop those questions and doubts hounding me for ever. One thing I'm not even sure I should do or I can do. But which I do do.

I disregard Doug's briefing instructions and I stop being quiet.

'Hey! It's me! Over here! It's Sebastian! If you're in here, meet me outside. Now! It's Sebastian!'

My outburst really injects new life into Doug. The Force is suddenly with him. He puts me in a headlock and drags me, stumbling and tripping, up the steps to the exit. Some of the audience laugh at us. Most just stare. Chewbacca makes a weird screeching noise. Someone dressed as Yoda takes the opportunity to deliver a personal response.

'Yeah, I'll meet you outside, Sebastian. And punch ya friggin' head in, I will!'

This is met with whistles and cheers and a supportive round of applause. The empire is striking back. Doug finally pushes me through the doors out into the light where I trip and end up sitting on the carpet. I do a quick sweep of the foyer. Maybe *this* is my romcom moment!

Nuh.

'That's it, son. Time for you to leave, or you'll be in real strife!'

'Sorry, it's just I had to …'

'Everything okay here, Doug?'

Great. Now Nick has joined us. Somehow he has managed to temporarily pry himself away from Jodie long enough to lend a hand with the troublemaker. He looks particularly irritated by his forced separation.

'Yeah, I'm good. This joker is just leaving. Aren't you, pal?'

I hold up my hands in surrender and agree willingly. Why would I want to stay, anyway? All my questions have been answered. Just not the way I wanted them to be. I get to my feet and begin the dead man walking journey to the good old sliding doors with Doug and Nick either side for company.

I feel embarrassed and beaten and confused, but at least I've done everything I can. I've looked everywhere, and she's definitely not here.

Unless …

We're passing the men's toilet. I only notice because the door actually says *Leading Men* and it has a weird silhouette on it of someone's head who I'm probably supposed to recognise but don't. George Clooney, perhaps? Up ahead is a second door labelled *Leading Ladies,* with another mysterious silhouette on it. I was wrong. There's still one other place she might be.

I deliberately increase my pace. My two bodyguards Doug and Nick up theirs as well to stay with me. We stride past the Ladies on our left. I wait till we've gone a few paces further on before I hit the brakes. As my escorts overrun me, I spin round and charge back the way we've come. By the time Doug and Nick react, it's too late. I'm already at the Leading Ladies door (is that Marilyn Monroe?) with my shoulder and head wedged inside and my voice bouncing and echoing around the white tiles.

'It's me! Sebastian! I'm here! At the start! Meet me outside! Now! It's …'

A strangled scream comes from inside. Suddenly I'm not being guided or escorted any more. I'm being yanked back out into the foyer and pushed, prodded and forcibly propelled through the just-open-in-time sliding doors of the entrance.

Doug jabs an angry finger in my face.

'Don't you try to come back in here *ever*! You hear me, son?'

'Yeah. Piss off, arsehole!' Nick adds just for helpful clarification.

I step out into the twilight and straighten my clothes as the doors close behind me. Now Nick is the one jabbing his finger my way and mouthing something that doesn't look like 'Have a nice day!' Meanwhile Doug is busy speaking into a phone or walkie-talkie of some kind. I head down the steps and go far enough along the path to satisfy Nick and Doug that I'm not thinking of coming back and storming the men's toilet.

From where I'm standing, I can just make out the entrance doors through the branches of a tree. Nick and Doug are nowhere to be seen now. I stop and wait. Well, here it is. This is definitely my absolute last romcom moment opportunity. You know the kind of thing. It all looks done and dusted, and I've made a complete jerk of myself for no reason, but wait! She's actually heard me in the cinema or the ladies' loo and just when I'm about to give up all hope, I see a figure silhouetted in the entrance way and hear a voice calling out to me.

And right at that moment I do. I *do* hear a voice calling out to me.

'You again!'

Except it's not coming from the entrance. It's coming from behind me. Back up the path, the large, disturbingly familiar silhouette of Tomas Paonga is barrelling my way just like that big mother boulder in *Indiana Jones*.

Awwwww, shit ...

26. THE OTHER GUY

I back away a step or two as Tomas Paonga looms closer. I try a pre-emptive strike.

'Look, I'm not doing anything, okay? Just standing here minding my own business. That's all.'

Tomas isn't buying it, and he spells it out to me in his rumbling, chopped-up voice. 'Minding your own business, eh? Shouting in the movies. Breaking into the Ladies. Disturbing the patrons.'

Well, at least now I know who Doug was busy reporting to on the phone just before.

'Okay, I can explain. They got that all wrong.'

'Sure they did.'

'It's true. I wasn't trying to cause any trouble. I was just trying to find someone, that's all.'

'Me too. You. Now we get to hang out together for a bit, eh.'

He jerks his head at the path behind him. 'Start walking.'

'Walking? Where're we going?'

'*You're* going home and *I'm* showing you the way out.'

'No, wait. You don't understand. I can't leave. Not yet. I can't.'

And then I go just that *little* bit too far.

'I *won't!*'

Tomas Paonga's small, dark eyes bore into me. His curled-up lip curls more. He lowers his face dangerously close to mine.

'What was that you just said?'

It's too late to take it back. I have to do something. He's

blocking the path, so I attempt to push past him. It's pointless. It's like trying to push past a building. Nothing moves. Well, not entirely nothing. A big hand encircles my bicep like it's a broom handle. A broom handle that's being crushed in a vice.

What do I do now? Stand my ground? How? I haven't *got* any ground. Tomas Paonga is hogging it all! Challenge him to a fight? Man Mountain versus Boy Molehill. How do we decide the winner? Best out of three deaths? It's a no-contest. I'm beaten before I start. All I can throw at him is the truth. So I throw it with all the strength I have left.

'Look. Tomas. Please. It's the girl, okay? You remember the girl? The one who was there with me and the fire extinguisher? White hair? Shaved head? Earrings? That's who I'm trying to find. Her. She left this message for me and I *thought* it meant that she was going to be in the movie theatre somewhere. But I was wrong and now I've got no idea where she is. Honestly, that's all I was trying to do. Find her. I'm not crazy. I wasn't trying to be smart or cause any trouble. I didn't mean to upset anyone or anything like that. But I had to make sure I hadn't missed her. That's what all the shouting and the ladies' loo thing was about. I was just trying to find the girl.'

He releases his grip from my arm but the dead eyes squaring me off remain lifeless. The mouth stays curled. Then a word rumbles out of it.

'Zoe.'

'Sorry, what?'

'The girl. Zoe.'

And then I remember.

'Ah, yeah, that's the one. Zoe. Sure. Her. I'm trying to find her.'

'Why?'

'Because … okay… because she's upset and I'm worried about her, Tomas. And because I … well, I like her, okay? I like her a lot.'

Until I say it out aloud, until I put it into words, I don't realise how true it might be.

'Please. Just let me keep looking for her. That's all I'm asking. I won't cause any more trouble. Just don't make me leave. Not yet. Don't be the guy that does that. The guy that ruins everything. Don't be that guy, Tomas, please. Be the other guy.'

I pick up some small movement in those dark, pea-like eyes, and the rough globe of Tomas Paonga's head tilts a tiny bit my way.

'What *other* guy?'

'The guy who understands. The guy who helps. You know, like in those romcom movies?'

Tomas's face is about as animated as a blob of cooled lava.

'Yeah, well, no, I haven't seen many either, obviously. But in the couple I've been *forced* to watch sometimes there's these scenes mainly towards the end, where some guy is desperately trying to find the girl – or vice versa – so they can finally be together, but she's about to get on a plane and leave his life forever and go back to Hollywood or she's in some important meeting or on a train platform or at the top of the Empire State Building or about to be married or go off with someone else. You get the idea. Anyway, the thing is, the guy's *so* close to finding her but then, right at the last minute, he can't get to her because some official or cop is blocking his way and won't let him through or maybe the place is closed or there's a massive traffic jam or his car breaks down or something. But just when it looks like it's all over and the guy will lose the girl forever, what usually happens is that someone sees how important it is for those two people to get together, and they end up doing something to help out. Like maybe they give them a police escort or a lift on their motorbike or they bend the rules or they just look the other way or something.'

All the time I'm rambling on, the face I'm straining my neck to look up at is unflinching. Never has the expression 'talking to a brick wall' seemed so real to me. I haven't got much left to give, but I give it everything I have.

'Well, *this* is like one of those moments for me. I need to find the girl, Tomas. She's angry and hurt and upset and it's my fault. All my fault. And it will not stand. It cannot stand. I won't let it stand. I didn't mean to upset her, but I was stupid and I did and I'm sorry and now I have to make that better. I *have* to. But I can't do that if I get thrown off campus because I'm sure she's still here somewhere only so far I'm doing a really, really crap job of finding her. So right now I could do with a break. I need something to go my way. I need someone to be on my side. Someone who gets it. And if I'm going to have any chance of finding the girl, then right here and right now, I need *you*, Tomas, to be that guy for me. Please.'

Tomas Paonga is as silent and still as a cement pylon until his nostrils flare out and he sniffs in some air. He raises his right hand above my head. I have to fight to stop myself from cringing. His index finger uncurls from his fist and he rotates it in slow circles.

'I will be around,' he says in his base-drum voice. 'Remember that. And if I hear of any trouble from you. Any trouble. Then I won't be the guy who understands. I won't even be the guy who shows you off the campus. Do you want to know what guy I will be?'

I really don't want to know, but somehow I get the feeling that he's mighty keen to tell me, and I think it would be terribly impolite not to let him, and terribly impolite is the very last thing I want to be to Tomas Paonga right now.

'No. No idea. What guy would you be, then?'

For the first time a smile crawls onto Tomas Paonga's face. It doesn't really warm my heart. His massive head closes in on my ear like a hovering death star.

'I'll be the guy who *says* he's going to show you off the campus but takes you someplace nice and quiet along the way and beats the shit out of you. *That's* the guy I will be.'

The smile dies. It's not a great loss. I'm not convinced it was alive to begin with.

'Now you tell me,' Tomas Paonga says, sounding out each word like a death knell, 'are *you* the guy who understands *that*?'

I can't bounce my head up and down fast or often enough.

'Oh, yeah, that's me. No worries. I'm that guy, all right. I was *born* that guy!'

It takes time for my internal organs to unknot themselves enough before I fully realise what's just happened and what it means.

'So … you're saying … you're saying that you're going to let me stay, right? You're *not* going to make me leave? Is that what you're saying?'

Tomas Paonga doesn't even bother answering. He's through speaking. He just repeats his rotating finger sign to remind me of his last words then he twirls slowly around like a small planet before setting off down the path to resume his silent orbiting of the campus.

'Hey, thanks, man! Thanks, Tomas!' I call after him. 'You *are* that guy! You are that *awesome* guy! You will *always* be that guy to me, Tomas! Always!'

I can't believe what's just happened. Something's *finally* gone my way. But then the reality of the situation hits me, and my excitement and relief fade quickly. The fact is that probably ten minutes have passed since I was thrown out of the cinema, and even though I survived a second, far-too-close encounter with Tomas Paonga, I'm still standing here alone.

I look back to the entrance. Night is falling fast now and the inside lights are spilling through the glass doors and down the steps. But that's all that's happening. There's no familiar silhouette in the entrance. There's no one calling out to me. There's no sign whatsoever of any kind of a happy feel-good ending here.

I text Tolly. *No luck. Coming back.*

I take my final look at those sliding doors. Well, you can't say I didn't try. How more 'back to the start' could I possibly get? Here I am, standing around like a dork, doing *exactly* what I was doing six or seven hours ago. Gawking at a stupid set of sliding doors waiting for a girl to come through them. And just to complete the dismal re-enactment, an old, reliable mantra returns to keep me company. Except this time it feels so perfect and so appropriate and so absolutely spot-on, that I can't help but say the words out loud. 'What a sad, pathetic prick you are.'

And a voice drifts down to me from above.

'You want to be careful, you know. I hear they lock people up who go about talking to themselves.'

I twist round. There's a high retaining wall behind me. At the top is a yellow railing. A girl is leaning over it. At first I can't make out her face because the lamplight above her is shining in my eyes. Then she moves to block it and she's no longer a mysterious silhouette. I can see her clearly now, smiling down at me with the light forming a soft halo around her hair. It's what my Film and Television teacher would call 'the Money Shot'.

It's also a rolled-gold, top-shelf, classic romcom moment if ever there was one.

I smile back up at her.

Of all the sad, pathetic lives, of all the sad, pathetic pricks, in all the sad, pathetic world, she walks into mine.

'Helena,' I say. 'Hi.'

27. THE REJECTS

I climb the steps to where she's standing. I've forgotten how perfect she is. It's hard to believe that we both share the same world, let alone this same small piece of university ground.

'Hi, yourself. What were you mumbling about down there, anyway?'

'Nothing important.'

'No? You didn't seem very happy.'

'Well, I am now.'

The words are out of my mouth before I realise how they sound. Helena smiles and looks away from me briefly.

'So, how was *Casablanca*?'

'Different. But I liked it. How was … your movie?'

'*Fast and Ridiculous 52*? Let's just say that it lived down to my very low expectations. Although it's probably unfair for me to comment on the thing as a whole, because, well … I slept through big chunks of it.'

'What? You fell asleep? How is that even possible? Didn't the explosions, the car smashes, the screeching tyres and the shoot-outs keep you awake?'

'No, I think that's what put me to sleep. They just went on and on and on crashing over me. Like being by the ocean. You don't hear the waves after a while. It was Corban who kept me awake. Or tried to. Mostly with his elbow.'

The thought of that makes me laugh.

'I'm glad *you* think it's funny. Corbs certainly didn't. Got pretty worked up about it, actually. Apparently it wasn't so much the sleeping bit that upset him ... more the snoring.'

'Oh my god, there was snoring?'

'So I'm told. I can't confirm it one hundred per cent because I may have been asleep at the time.'

Now we're both laughing.

'Actually I shouldn't joke about it. We had quite the heated *discussion* when the movie was over.'

She stops and indicates the empty space around her.

'Which is why, as you can see, Corbs is no longer gracing us with his presence. Decided he'd rather go into town with his mates. I decided I'd rather not. Probably safe to say that it's unlikely we'll be seeing any more movies together. Or doing anything much else together, really.'

'Sorry to hear that,' I say automatically.

Helena lets a second pass before she asks the next question.

'Are you really?'

I feel her eyes on me and I hesitate a little before I answer.

'To tell you the truth, no. I never really liked him that much.'

She smiles.

'To tell *you* the truth, I don't blame you.'

The sound of bands tuning up carries down from the Great Court and helps cover the awkward pause we're caught in. Helena leans back against the rail.

'So, that explains why I'm alone. What about you? Where's your friend? Was it ... *Frida*?'

'Yeah,' I agree in order to avoid a long explanation. 'Ah, not really sure where she is. Been looking for her, actually. We sort of had a *discussion* as well. I haven't been able to find her. She might have gone home.'

'Really? Looks like we've both been abandoned, then.'

'Could be.'

Helena pushes herself off the rail.

'Well … I've been trying to make up my mind if I should head off or hang around for the Great Court concert. Some of my friends are there already. Sounds like it's starting up.'

She waits. I think she expects me to speak, but I'm not sure what to say, so she prompts me.

'Soooo, what about you, then? What are you doing now? Feel like checking out some bands too? Perhaps we rejects should stick together.'

And there it is. Cut into perfect little bite-sized bits and served up to me on a plate. The whole thing couldn't be more romcom-perfect if I'd written the script, chosen the setting, positioned the actors and directed the whole scene myself. And it's obvious what my next line should be.

Something simple and easy would do it, like 'Great idea. Let's go!'

Or perhaps I could try for a cute and witty line like 'A reject never rejects another reject. That's Rule One of Reject Law!'

So why am I saying *this* instead?

'Look, that'd be brilliant and I'd really like to, but … I'm sorry, I can't. There's something I have to do.'

Being rejected by a reject must be a whole new experience for Helena, but to her great credit she contains her astonishment well. Instead she lines me up with her almond eyes like she's looking down a camera lens.

'And it can't wait? This thing you *have* to do?'

There's part of me that wants to yell, 'Hell yes, for you, anything can wait!'

Just not a big enough part.

'Not really,' I say.

'I'm guessing it has something to do with your kindy buddy?'

'Yeah. It does. I really need to find her.'

'Rescuing her again, are you?'

Something about that suggestion gets to me.

'Actually, you know that story she told you? The one about me saving her from the bully? Well, it's not true. She just said that to make me look good. I'm no hero. Not brave enough. I've never saved anyone. Ever. If anyone's a hero, it's her. She's the hero. Not me.'

It's true. She saved me from dying of embarrassment with Helena. She saved me from the wrath of Tomas Paonga. She saved me from becoming a theatre sports casualty. She may have even saved me from Town Planning.

'Hero, eh?' Helena says. 'Sounds like she can take care of herself, then. So how come you need to find her so badly?'

I look at Helena. She really is a PFH. More than that in fact. And she's waiting for an answer. I give her a question instead.

'Have you ever seen the film *The Big Lebowski*?'

Naturally she looks at me like I've totally lost the romcom plot or accidently flipped over two pages of the script.

'Never heard of it. Why?'

I really don't have time to explain. Besides, maybe it's only part of the answer, anyway. And maybe not even the most important part.

'Doesn't matter,' is what I end up saying.

Helena is frowning. Can you blame her? Now she's shaking her head and smiling. Probably thinking that being rejected by someone who blurts out irrelevant and pointless questions might not be such a bad thing after all.

'Okaaaaaay, then. Well, on that *curious* note I think I'll call it a night. If I don't see you around somewhere in between, I might see you back here in what … a year and a bit?'

'Hope so.'

'Me too. You never know when I might need to borrow another pen.'

'Any time. I have your back. My stationery is your stationery.'

'Good to know.'

She looks at me again like I'm some abstract sculpture that doesn't quite make sense to her.

'Well, see ya.'

'Yeah. Bye.'

As she waves a hand my way, I remember something that I've been meaning to ask.

'Hey, Helena, has anyone ever told you that you look a lot like Taylor Swift?'

Her head flops back and she gives an exaggerated roll of her eyes.

'Ergh. Yeah, I get that a lot. Some of my so-called friends love teasing me about it. But I'm used to it now, so when anyone says anything or makes a joke about it, I just ...'

She wiggles her hips and flaps her hands by her sides in a well-known dance move.

'... try to ignore them.'

My heart starts to do that collapsing ice-shelf thing again. But holds. I laugh.

'I see what you did there,' I tell her.

She winks and I watch her walk away. Here's no longer looking at you, kid. Who knows, maybe in some alternative feel-good, romcom fantasy universe, I'm right there, walking alongside her.

But not here. Not in this crazy, mashed-up world of mine.

Here I'm jogging back to my best friend Tolly with a message ringing in my head that I'm determined to decipher.

28. THE ANSWER

When I get back, Tolly has finished off his muffins and an orange juice and is busy scrolling through something on his phone.

'No go?' he says as I collapse into the seat opposite him.

'Nuh. I looked everywhere. You *sure* you had that message right?'

'I'm not even going to dignify that with a reply,' he says as he blanks his screen. 'What took you so long, anyway?'

I give him the lowlights of my visit to the theatre. I edit out Helena.

'Impressive. Almost starting a riot during a screening of *Star Wars*, harassing women in the toilet, getting physically thrown out of a cinema and being threatened by a security guard. What a full and rich life you're leading. Wouldn't tell your parents about any of that.'

'Gee, ya think? Hey, thanks for warning me, Toll. I was going to write a blog about it, include some CCTV footage and send them a link.'

Tolly puts on a sickly smile and points at me.

'You're being sarcastic there, aren't you? You can't fool me. I can tell.'

I ignore him and focus on the real issue.

'I just don't get it. If you want to start again you must go back to the start. That's what she said, right? Well, I did that, didn't I? I was at the start. I did my bit. So why wasn't *she* there?'

Tolly sets his phone down on the table.

'Let's look at this calmly and logically. Is there anything else it could mean? Any other possible interpretations? Anything else it might be referring to? Anything at all?'

'That's what I've been trying to work out but I can't see what else it could be, can you?'

All I get in reply is silence and a screwed-up mouth.

'I don't know, Tolly. Maybe I've got it all wrong. Maybe she was just sharing some words of wisdom like one of those crappy motivational posters in our classroom. *To start again you must return to the start!* Maybe I'm not supposed to do anything at all.'

Tolly ponders that possibility.

'No, there's got to be more to it than just that. Don't forget, after she gave me the message she said she needed time to get somewhere. So that must mean that the start has to be a real, physical place.'

Yeah, that makes sense. But what physical place? I search my brain for possibilities.

'Hey, do you think maybe I'm supposed to *start* at the movies, which is where we first met, but then keep going? You know, retrace our steps and go to all the places we went to during the day? Like the cafeteria, that theatre sports place, where that Pitch Drop thing was, you know, all those places? Do you think if I do that, she'll meet me along the way somewhere? Could *that* be it?'

'Maaaaaaaybe,' Tolly says in a way that translates into, 'Only a crazy person would actually believe such a thing'.

'Well, *what* then? Come on, Mister Extreme Brain Training

program graduate. Fire up the old Tolly Cranium Super Computer. Help me out here. Give me *something*.'

He spreads his hands wide and gives me nothing except a pained look. My heart sinks to somewhere near my bladder. If Tolly is stumped, what chance do I have?

'You know what? Maybe she doesn't think you *can* start again once you've stuffed something up as badly as I did. Maybe sending me to an empty cinema was her way of getting revenge and teaching me a lesson. And *maybe* that "somewhere" she said she needed time to get to was as far away from me as possible.'

Tolly listens but doesn't comment on my theory or suggest any new ones of his own. He only speaks after his phone lights up with a new message.

'Dad. In a bit of traffic. Says he'll be at the pick-up point in about fifteen minutes.'

I watch him tap out a quick reply.

'So what are you going to do? Are you coming with us or staying?'

My mind was made up about that when I gave my answer to Helena. It's all or nothing now. With 'nothing' looming as the odds-on favourite.

'Staying. If I can't figure out what the message means, I'll just keep looking for her.'

Tolly strokes then pulls at the hairs on his chin, deep in thought about something or other.

'Tolly, be honest with me. Do you think I'm being an idiot?'

He takes my question seriously. A little too seriously.

'Let's see. Going berserk in a cinema. Mounting a siege on

the ladies' loos. I mean, once again the evidence pretty much speaks for itself, don't you think?'

Not really the supportive, confidence-boosting kind of answer I was hoping for. But he hasn't finished.

'However, I'm not sure that's the real question you should be asking yourself here.'

'No?' I say, losing my patience a little with him. 'So what do you think *is* the real question I should be asking myself here?'

Tolly leans his elbows on the table and taps the tips of his fingers together.

'The real question I think you should be asking yourself here, young Sebastian, is this: Is the *cause* of your idiocy worth being an idiot about?'

Key scenes and images from the day tumble through my mind as I consider Tolly's question. It doesn't take me long to find my answer.

'Yeah,' I tell him. 'Yeah, I think she is. I think she definitely is.'

Tolly smiles.

'I think you may be right, young man,' he says.

I feel like hugging him, but I don't.

'Thanks, Toll. But maybe if I was a little less of an idiot, I might be able to decode her message.'

Tolly taps out a rapid fingertip drum roll on the table top.

'Okay, look. I really need to go now, so if you've *definitely* made up your mind to stay, I might as well …'

I stick up a hand and cut him off mid-sentence. One of those key scenes I've just recalled has thrown up a strange thought in my brain.

'Wait on. Wait a minute. You don't think she could have meant … Tolly, quick, have you got the campus map on your phone?'

'Just deleted it,' he says, and immediately pulls a hard copy from his inside coat pocket. 'But here's one I prepared earlier.'

I snatch it from him and spread it on the table between us. 'Where would something like that be?' I mumble to myself as I search the legend for buildings and facilities. 'Maybe on the oval somewhere … or … or wait … they wouldn't have an *actual* …'

I check the legend again. They do. I find exactly what I'm looking for. They have an actual …

'That's it! That's gotta be what she meant. The start. Has to be!'

I'm already pushing my chair back to leave when Tolly makes use of his sizeable wing span and latches on to my arm.

'Hold on. What is it? Where are you going? Show me exactly.'

I stab a finger at the map.

'There! N9. Back to the start!'

Tolly examines where I'm pointing then double-checks the reference in the legend. He grins. He gets it straightaway. Of course he does. He's Tolly.

'Not bad for an idiot,' he says as he disentangles his long limbs from the chair and table. 'Right. My work here is done.'

I collect all my gear and I'm ready to go too. But I'm stalling. Tolly notices.

'Problem?'

Yeah. There is. The last time I just rushed off like a mad man.

But what happened at the cinema and the stuff with Tomas, and particularly Helena, have made me think a lot more about what I'm actually doing and about the girl I'm hoping to find.

'It's just ... that story ... what happened at the party ... If all that stuff she said about herself ... about her life ... if it's all true ... then ... then what do I do when I find her? What do I say to her? How do I help? I mean, I can't make it better or make it go away. Nothing I can do will change *anything*.'

Tolly stands in front of me. 'Probably not,' he says, then presses a large, bony fist against my chest. 'But if you want my advice, do it anyway.'

29. THE START

I leave Tolly and jog along the ring road then follow a loop down towards the playing fields. When I pass the sports pavilion I take the next left turn. Up ahead I see a low-set building surrounded by a chest-high, tubular steel fence. When I get to it, there's just enough nearby street lighting for me to read the sign out front.

University Kindergarten
Operating Hours: Mon to Fri 8 am to 5 pm

It's been a bit of a roundabout journey, but I think I've finally arrived at the start.

There's only a small garden and a short pathway leading to the main entrance so I follow the fence around to the rear of the building. It backs on to bushland. It's just the kind of 'quiet place' Tomas Paonga might choose to carry out his threat. I push that thought from my mind and inspect the back of the kindergarten more closely.

What I see is a large outdoor play area partly covered by three triangular shade cloths. With daylight almost gone, large sections of it are just vague shapes and shadows. The last thing I want to do is invite Tomas Paonga to join me, so I quickly decide against even a drastically toned-down encore of my vocal performance from the cinema. Instead I lower my backpack inside, take a firm grip on the fence and hoist myself up. With two hands and a foot poised on the top railing and my other foot braced halfway up for balance, I steady myself for a leap into the semi-darkness.

The manic thumping of my heart is now almost drowning out the clubbing beat floating down from the Great Court. Am I really going to do this? Am I going to add 'illegal entry into a kindergarten' to my already comprehensive list of idiocy for the day? What would my parents be feeling if they could see me right now? How much fear and worry would I be responsible for putting in their eyes? The more I think about it, the more my centre of balance shifts to the outside of the fence. Until I remember Tolly's question. The one he said I should ask myself. The answer is still the same. I lean forward, raise my other foot to the top rail and push off.

The artificial turf I land on is soft and spongy. I crouch there and brace myself for the sirens to blare out and for an enraged Tomas Paonga to sweep through and crash tackle me like the human wrecking ball that he was born to be. But neither of those things happen, so I collect my bag, stand up and carefully edge my way ahead.

Until security lights blaze on and two blinding white blotches are implanted on my retinas.

I panic and stumble forward. One of my hands collides with what I assume are wooden paint easels and they crash and clatter to the ground. Once again I prepare for the siren blast and for a totally pissed-off Tomas Paonga to pin me to the ground like a bug in an insect display. But again, nothing happens. I stay where I am this time and blink my eyes until the white blotches dissolve away. With the spotlights on, the once hidden sections of the play area are now visible.

And I've found what I was looking for.

In the corner of the yard, boxed in on each side by wooden logs, is a sandpit. A girl is sitting hunched over in the rectangle of white sand. Her arms are wrapped tightly around her legs and the side of her head is resting on her raised knees. A curtain of white hair hangs down over her face. On the sand beside her are a bag and a pair of sandals.

She straightens up when I approach and pushes the hair from her face. There's a red line on her right cheek caused by a fold in her skirt.

'You know, if only I had two good ears,' she says to me, 'I might have heard you coming.'

'Yeah, well, I can't believe they allow kids in here. The place is a death trap.'

I smile. Uneasily.

'Ah, you don't think maybe we should leave now? I've got an idea that there's some weird law against breaking into places that don't belong to you. Plus, you probably didn't notice, but *somebody* just made the lights come on.'

'Sit,' is all she says.

'But it's just that if that security guy finds …'

Now she's holding up a finger and patting the patch of sand to her left. I step over the wooden log border and sit down beside her. A few seconds pass before we are both flooded by shadows.

'There,' she says. 'Now as long as you don't jump up and down or wave your arms about or charge around crashing into stuff like a wounded rhino, they stay off.'

'Got it.'

It goes quiet then while I try to work out what I should say next. She beats me to it by stating the obvious.

'So … you found me, then.'

'Yeah. Yes, I did. Well … *even*tually.'

Silence once more. I break it this time.

'I mean, I don't want to be critical here, but do you think *maybe* you could have made that message you gave Tolly just a *tiny* bit clearer? You know, something like … "Tell Sebastian if he wants to start again, I'll be sitting in a sandbox down at the university kindergarten". Now *that* I might have worked out *almost* straightaway.'

She smiles a little but there's no real joy behind it.

'Sorry about that. Wasn't really sure if I wanted to be found. Besides, I couldn't make it too easy. Had to weed out all those town planner types, didn't I?'

Another town planner dig. But I don't mind any more. At least she's talking to me.

'Right. Well, I think maybe I should hang on to my town planner membership card for a bit longer, because I was lucky to make the cut. Actually, forget that. I was lucky to make it here alive.'

She turns my way.

'What does that mean?'

'Remember your friend Tomas from security? Well, he kindly offered – and I'm quoting here – to "beat the shit" out of me, and there are a couple of guys working at the Hub that I know for sure would have happily joined in.'

'What? Are you serious? Why?'

'Well, *apparently* it's not the done thing to yell out like a whack job during a movie screening or while attempting to infiltrate the ladies' loo. Now wouldn't you think they'd have signs up explaining stuff like that?'

A pair of wide, bewildered eyes are on me now. They seemed to be assessing my sanity and almost certainly finding it wanting.

'You *did* that? Why would you do something like that?'

I take a deep breath to help me get through this.

'Because *you* said to go back to the start and *I* thought the cinema was the start, didn't I, seeing how, you know, that's sort of where we *started*. Well, anyway, then I guess I overstayed my welcome and was asked to leave and never return, but I sort of couldn't do that until I made a hundred per cent sure you weren't in there somewhere.'

'By yelling out in the cinema and the ladies' loo?'

'Believe it or not, they actually seemed like good ideas at the time.'

She gives her head a sharp shake and blinks her eyes like she's taken a swig of something potent.

'Wow. You seriously better hope the Town Planning Standards Committee never finds out about this.'

She stares at her feet and begins to wiggle her toes down into the sand.

'So, did you actually figure out the message all by yourself … or did Tolly help you?'

'Tolly? Mr Almost-a-Genius? He was hardly any help at all.

If I hadn't finally worked it out, you would have been sitting around alone all night.'

'Nothing new there,' she says. 'But you're wrong. That wouldn't have happened. I knew you'd find me. If you really wanted to.'

Her confidence in me is refreshing but ridiculous.

'How could you *possibly* be sure of that?'

She pushes sand up over her feet and ankles and pats it down.

'Because I told Tolly where I'd be.'

I swivel round to see if she's kidding. It's clear that she's not. Only my fear of triggering the lights again stops me from jumping up and down, waving my arms about and charging around crashing into stuff like a wounded rhino.

'What? Tolly knew? All the time I was busting my brain trying to figure it out, asking for his help, Tolly *knew*? Then why the hell didn't he tell me?'

'Because I said he could only tell you if you really wanted to find me but you couldn't work it out on your own.'

Suddenly a lot of things about Tolly's attitude and behaviour make sense.

'Geez, he really pushed that to the limit, didn't he? Just wait till I see him tomorrow.'

She turns on me.

'Hey, you leave Tolly alone, okay? He just did what I asked him to do.'

She pauses then and takes a breath before nailing me to the wall.

'Which, in my experience, is not something that everybody

does.'

That comment slams a door shut on all our previous conversation and turns the lock on everything else except the words I came here to say.

'I'm sorry,' I tell her. 'About the card thing. I really am. I shouldn't have looked. It was wrong. I don't know why I ... doesn't matter ... It was just a really shitty thing to do, that's all. I acted like a dick. Just like Vogel. But I didn't mean to upset you. That's the last thing ... I'm sorry.'

She's staring at her feet packed in sand. She arches and wiggles her toes and they break through the surface like hatching turtles.

'Okay,' she says finally. 'But you're nothing like Vogel. He's never sorry.'

The silence swirls and closes in around us once again. Tighter and more urgent now, like it's waiting on the question that I'm almost too afraid to ask. I look out through the gaps in the shade cloths at the clear night sky. I can see a few bright stars and an almost full moon. It's nice, but it doesn't make the question in my head any easier to put into words.

'What ... you said before ... up in the Great Court ... about that party ... and Karen Kratzman ... All that stuff about her life and what happened to her ... Was that ... is that ... all true?'

I can hear the sound of shallow breathing beside me. My own breathing has stopped. The answer creeps through in a worn and tattered whisper.

'The whole truth ... and nothing but the truth ...'

I turn to see a bitter smile cutting into her face.

'... so *didn't*-help-me, god.'

30. THE TRUTH

For the first time today, I want her to be lying to me. I want it all to be one of her plucked-from-the-air stories. I want to prove her wrong.

'But the cigarettes … You said there were …'

I don't finish the sentence. She looks across at me and I point a finger at the inside of my forearm.

She stares at it without replying. Then she leans forward and stretches her arms out in front. Her white cotton top rides up at the back. Even in the shadows there's enough moonlight falling on her pale skin to see the small, dark circles it reveals. A putrid wave of realisation and anger washes over me. 'Jesus, I … I'm …'

But what can I really say? That I'm sorry? That I know what it's like? That it's all okay now because I'm going to somehow magically make everything better? They're all just empty, useless words, plucked from some stupid, feel-good, romcom script. What good are they to her now?

She sits back and doesn't wait for me to find my voice.

'You know, I never saw her again. That girl at the party. The one I spilled my guts to. No idea who she was. I wish I did.'

She smooths out a patch of sand and writes a K on it with the tip of a white fingernail.

'That party was … a low point. For me.'

'Hey, look, you don't have to …'

I'm not sure if what I'm trying to say is for her sake or for mine, but I'm cut off anyway.

'Vogel. He was there that night. In that group of boys. The ones I was warned about.'

She digs her fingers deep under the letter she's written and scoops it up in a clump of sand.

'He had plenty of stories to tell about me at school on Monday.'

She spreads her fingers and lets the sand slip through them.

'Not all of them were lies.'

A tightness claws at my chest and throat. I want to say something to her but I still can't find the words that will make any difference. She sees me struggling and comes to my rescue. Again. Her voice is more cheerful and upbeat now, as if I'm the one who needs comforting and reassuring.

'But, on the bright side, only one more semester of putting up with deadbeats like Vogel and I'll be at Kingston.'

I look her way and she pushes out a tired smile.

'Yeah, believe it or not, the boarding scholarship story is actually true too. Got it through some charity thing. You just had to be smart enough, poor enough and screwed up enough to win one. I ticked all the boxes.'

She starts raking the sand over her feet again while she talks.

'My auntie made me apply for it. My mum's sister. Didn't even know I had any relatives till she tracked me down this year. Found some letters or something. I could be moving in with her. Have to be better than the shit hole they have me in now, I suppose. But I'm not sure about it. Or her. I have these "trust issues", apparently. That's one thing all the counsellors have agreed on. Go figure.'

I wonder about that 'shit hole' where she's living, but I don't ask. I'm through with interrogations. I'm not about to pound on any doors. So I just wait. And listen.

She pats down the high mound of sand piled over her feet, leaving a criss-cross of finger marks on the surface. Then she stops and looks off to where the lights in the centre of the university are glowing. Her eyes reflect the passion that blazes in her voice.

'I just want to get *here*, that's all. That's my goal. Study my arse off at Kingston next year and get to this place. I feel different here. Lighter. More alive. It's like I can be whoever I want to be here. Maybe even be me. Just need to get here first. Then I'm going to do what your Nanna Rose said. Start turning the pages. Start burying the past.'

The fire in her eyes flares and holds on briefly, then dims.

'Well that's the plan, anyway. Trouble is, I've tried that turning pages thing before and every time the new pages have ended up being just as shitty as the old ones. Sometimes even shittier.'

She pushes out those last words like they've left a bad taste in her mouth.

'Might need to ask Nanna Rose what her secret is.'

I know I should speak. I know I should say the words to challenge hers and take away some of their sadness and pain. But what are they? It's like I'm struck dumb on some real-life theatre sport stage with a spotlight shining on me and the audience restless with waiting.

She scoops up a handful of sand and throws it at the logs that border the sandpit.

'Hey, I think I've figured it out,' she says with little enthusiasm. 'Nana Rosa's secret. You know what I should do? I should get myself a *real* photo album like that one she had. You know, one of those old-fashioned ones where you stick the photos in. Maybe *that's* been my problem from the start. Just think about it. Digital photos on your phone or hanging around up in the cloud are never going to work, are they? How can you bury anything with those? You obviously need to be flipping over *real* pages, filled with *real* happy-snap memories. How stupid am I? That's clearly what I've been doing wrong all this time. So there you go. Problem solved. Happy days.'

The fake smile she has forced on to her lips weakens until it twists into a crooked line. She hugs her legs to her chest and rests her forehead on her knees. Her voice, when it comes, is barely more than a worn murmur.

'Of course, getting those happy snaps in the first place, even virtual ones for a virtual album, that's the hard part. That's always been the hard part for me.'

And at last I find them – the words I need to say to her. The words I *want* to say to her. But they're risky words to speak out loud. Dangerous words to let loose. Words that I know could turn on me, and hurt me.

I say them anyway.

31. The Words

'Maybe I could help you make them.'

There's no reaction. She remains locked in her knee-hugging position like a tight cocoon.

'What I mean is, if you needed to make some new memories … better ones … for those happy snaps you talked about … I just thought maybe I could help you with them … help you make them … if that was something you'd be okay with … or want.'

Still nothing. I know she can hear me, because her good ear is facing my way, so I keep talking. It's all I can do now.

'And not just me. Tolly too. Tolly would help, for sure. He'd *want* to help. I know he would. He helped me after Connor. A lot. And you know how much you love Tolly, right? So it wouldn't be just me. It'd be both of us helping. Tolly and me. And we're like superheroes, remember? You said so yourself.'

Still no movement. Still no sound. There's nothing else I can think of to do except to go on rapid-firing my words at her and hope that some might find their way through.

'And you know what? Maybe you don't even have to wait till you get to uni or even till next year when you're at Kingston to make new memories. Better ones. Maybe you've started making them already. Yeah, that's right. I mean, think about it. We've made some pretty good memories even today, haven't we? Like, you know, what about seeing the Pitch Drop Experiment? Now that was a life-changing event if ever there was one. Nobody could be the same after witnessing something like that. It's just not possible. I mean, we were there, right there, all three of us, you, me and Tolly, when like … *nothing* happened. Nothing at all. And we had front row seats to not see it when it didn't happen. How many people can say that? Man, I just had some trouble saying it myself. So yeah, the whole Pitch Drop thing, that's got to be worth a happy snap or two of memories for your album, doesn't it?'

Movement. At last. She loops her hair behind her good ear and rests her opposite cheek back on her knees. Her eyes open now and she's watching me. And waiting.

Words. I need more words. They're all I've got.

'And um … what about how you and Tolly killed it at theatre sports? There's a heap of photos for your album right there. A couple of pages' worth at least. Oh, and don't forget how on this very day, you were the first person in the history of the world to figure out Tolly's name. That was genius. And you got crowned the Queen of Cleverdick-ed-ness, for crying out loud. Now *that's* got to go in. Have to have a shot of that. And … um … oh my god … how could I forget? Tolly giving it to Vogel in that lecture theatre in front of all those people. How about a full-page enlargement of Vogel's face when Tolly told him to stop being a dick for that one? And what about … um … Wait, what about …'

I've been rambling on like a crazy person, but now I'm spluttering on empty as my words are drying up. She's still waiting.

'… Yeah, another one could be … um …'

Her eyes are drifting away from me. I'm losing her.

'… What about …'

Her eyes return.

'You playing your song?'

Her voice is so quiet and ragged, I'm not certain I've heard what she's said.

'Sorry?'

She clears her throat and repeats it. Louder this time.

'That could be another one. You playing your song for me.'

I'll take it. I'll take anything at this point.

'Ah, sure. Sure, if you want. You could definitely have a shot of that. It's your album and clearly there's no accounting for personal taste …'

'You getting in trouble with the security guy and me saving your butt?'

'Yeah … I *guess* … but why …'

'Tolly crushing you in the drone challenge?'

'Wait. What? Not sure "crushing" is *quite* the word you're looking for.'

She lifts her head off her knees and places her chin back there instead.

'What about things that I didn't actually see? Things I wasn't there for. Like you looking for me in the cinema and doing all that weird psycho stuff and getting yourself thrown out? Could I put that in too even though I wasn't there when it happened?'

'Like I said, it's entirely up to you, but just remember you don't have to put *everything* in the album, you know. Just the really good stuff.'

'Oh no, I'd *definitely* want that in.'

And then the meaning behind her words finally filters through to me.

'Wait. Are you saying that you'd be okay with … with what I said about making new memories … and with me helping … and Tolly?'

She's staring at me. Shadows of fear and doubt are dancing in her eyes. I know that look.

'Maybe,' she says finally. 'But only on one condition.'

'Sure. Anything. What is it?'

'That I get to help you too.'

And now I'm totally confused.

'Help me? Help me with what?'

Her pale grey-green eyes are lining me up. She takes her time as if she's making sure her words are all in order.

'Help you to be something more than just *not your brother*.'

I'm not prepared to hear those words. And I'm not prepared either for tears that are swelling and stinging my eyes and threatening to spill out. I push my tongue hard against the roof of my mouth to hold them back. I win that battle, but I don't trust my voice to make solid enough sounds, so when I can, I just nod my agreement at her.

She leans her chin back on her knees and stares straight ahead.

'Now tell me why.'

It's another one of those vague questions she seems to like to ask.

'Why what?'

'Why everything. Why you're here? Doing all this. Saying

these *things* to me.'

I'm done with secrets. Maybe truth is the only thing that can survive between us now.

'It's pretty simple. I'm here because I want to be here. And I want to be here because you're here and I like being anywhere you are. Even theatre sports. Because I like *you*. The real you. Whoever that is.'

Her eyes begin to glisten and she turns her face away from me and rests the side of her head on her knees. An car crowded with metal piercings now faces the stars and the little silver moons dangling from her lobe are catching and reflecting the real moonlight above.

'And I'm *also* here,' I say softly, 'because you have no idea how beautiful you are. And it will not stand.'

She sits back up and uses the palms of both hands to wipe the moisture from beneath her eyes.

'Sorry, what was that?'

I smile at her.

'Nothing,' I say.

But it's not nothing. It's just about everything.

32. THE PHOTO

She stares at me a moment before kicking the sand off her feet. Then she stands up and waves her arms about until the spotlights blink back on.

'Okay, let's do this before I chicken out. Then maybe we could go and check out those bands I can half hear.'

I'm following her lead and getting to my feet as I ask my question.

'Do what?'

'What you came here to do. Start again. That's if you still want to.'

'I do,' I tell her. 'I definitely do.'

'Right, then. Let the official Starting Again ceremony begin.'

She faces me, sucks in a breath and holds out her right hand.

'Hi. I'm …'

She gives her head a little shake as if she can't believe the crazy thing she's about to do.

'… I'm Karen.'

I move my hand towards hers.

'Hi, Karen. I'm …'

I pull my hand away.

'Wait,' I say and dig out my phone. 'If we're going to make it really official, we need to record it.'

She doesn't seem totally against this idea so I set my phone to camera and hold it out in front of us with my finger positioned over the shutter button. We move closer together and I frame the shot as best I can.

'Take two,' I announce, and she offers her hand again.

'Hi. I'm Karen.'

Her voice is stronger and more certain now.

'Hi, Karen,' I say, and for the second time I move my hand towards hers. 'I'm …'

Her eyes lock on mine and she raises her eyebrows as she waits.

'… I'm Seb,' I tell her.

She smiles, and just as our hands join, I touch my finger lightly to the screen, then bring the phone in.

We both inspect the result.

'Nice,' she says.

It is. In the photo we're looking at each other and smiling. And our hands are joined. That's probably my favourite part. Of course, in reality they were only like that for a second or two before they parted. But the photo tells a different story. There, they never let go. I like that story better. And as someone once said, what's so great about reality, right?

And speaking of reality.

'So it was true after all,' I say. 'We met in a kindergarten sandpit.'

She pulls a face as if I've just declared the Earth to be round.

'Of course. Would I lie to you about something like that?'

'Apparently not. And now there's even photographic proof.'

'That's right. I'll have to get a copy. Here, let me have another look.'

She takes my phone and examines the shot more closely.

I watch as her smile grows wider at first, but then weakens and begins to slide from her face. She lifts a hand to the little hanging moons on her bad ear and glances up at me. Those fear and doubt shadows are back in her eyes. But there's something else there as well.

Karen Kratzman presses a row of small, white teeth into her bottom lip and crinkles up her eyes like she's preparing to be hit.

Her fingers clasp the tiny moons as she finds her voice.

'You maybe want to go photo-album shopping with me sometime?' she asks.

And just like that, a door finally slides open and of all the crazy mashed-up lives, of all the crazy mashed-up people, in all the crazy mashed-up world, she walks into mine.